D1452872

Scott Wiser

Cirque De Solitude

Written & Illustrated by Scott Wiser

Published by Scott Wiser LLC
Printed in China by Regent Publishing Services

Text and Illustrations by Scott Wiser
Editors: Rebecca Wiser, Wendy Wiser
Special Thanks to: Isaac Stewart, Travis Howe, David Wilson,
Mike Caudillo, Nathan A. Stout

The text for this book is set in Minion Pro, Doriel, Avenir, and University Roman Std Bold. The illustrations for this book were rendered in Adobe Photoshop.

Library of Congress Cataloging-In-Publication Data
Wiser, Scott, 1984 -
Cirque De Solitude / written and illustrated by Scott Wiser
Summary: Audra Jones, a timid 45-year-old woman, buys a private island only to discover it is already inhabited by circus people.
1st Edition
ISBN-13: 978-0-9863558-3-7
ISBN-10: 0-9863558-3-6
PCN: 2019902813

To All The Remarkable
Women In My Life

Cirque de Solitude

THE
CIRCUS ELEPHANT
LUCY ROSE

Chapter 1: A Morning Expedition

A limousine leaves the city and bumps along on an old dirt road. The mountain slips in and hides the city from view. Through the passenger window, sunrise lights flicker onto a cart stacked with worn, hardbound books.

Audra Jones's 42-year-old dainty hand reaches down and lifts the most tattered book of all. With her other hand, she strokes the gold-flecked remains of the classic embossed title: *The Circus Elephant*.

With her face buried in the pages of the open book, she inhales the sweet smell of years past. Her eyelashes flutter at the memories flooding her mind. Her eyes closely scan the first page of chapter three. The words and pictures spring to life in her imagination:

THE CIRCUS ELEPHANT

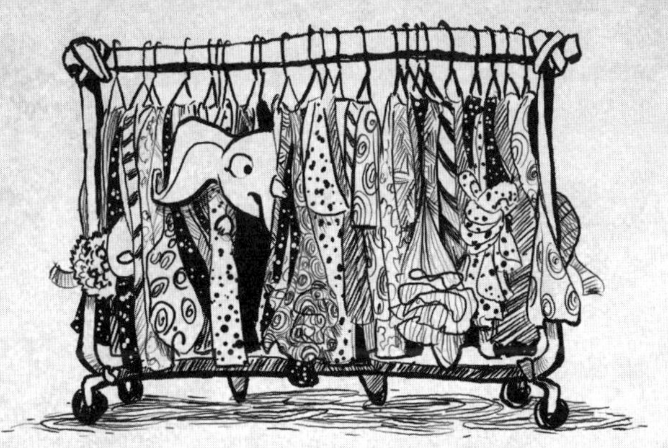

Elphie snuck back around
When the chimps were all gone.
She thirsted for water
From that small circus pond.

As her trunk touched the water
In the shade of nightfall,
Chimpy jumped out
On his big circus ball.

She froze, held her breath,
Hoping he wouldn't see,
As he whizzed about,
All balanced and free.

For a moment she marveled
At his agile tricks,
As he reveled and floated,
Through spins and kicks.

But when their eyes met
Elphie whimpered and bolted.
Round corners, more monkeys,
In zig-zags, she jolted.

She hid until midnight,
When no one was near.
Then hopped up on top of
Her own circus sphere.

At first she fumbled,
But with time she flew.
She balanced, She bounded,
And outside of her view...

Sneaky Chimpy rolled in
With glee in his grin.
He mirrored her gestures.
He danced like her twin.

Elphie's trance was enhanced,
As she posed so grand.
So Chimpy leapt forward,
Held onto her hand.

For a moment they balanced,
Suspended in air, and
When Elphie saw Chimpy
She chose not to care.

They leaped up together.
They swung from trapeze.
Launched out of a cannon
And cheered in the breeze.

They walked off in friendship,
A bond that transcends.
Feeling fearless, of course,
Until she met his friends...

Chuckling softly, Audra pulls the book to her chest and looks out the window. The sunlight waltzes away from the leafy branches and hides behind glowing morning fog. Her heart aches as she longs to be someplace else, someplace fantastical, not stuck in the passenger seat because she never learned to drive, not needing to interact with anyone at all, even her kind-hearted driver, Norman.

Moments after the limo stops, the front door opens. Norman stumbles out of the driver's seat and hurries back to open Audra's door. Dust and fog pour in through the limo door. Norman offers his hand. At sight of his hand, Audra pauses in hesitation. But since he's always so polite, how could she choose to reject the gesture?

Gingerly, Audra places her gloved hand in his and steps out, her face hidden beneath her tulip-garnished hat. As she turns back to pull out her book cart and basket, Norman pulls a rose from behind his back. He extends the rose toward her with an eager expression. Afraid that she may give him an awkward reaction, she pretends she doesn't see the rose, ducks under his arm and hurries off into the fog.

With a whimpered grunt, Norman tosses the rose into the back seat, shuts the door, and sulks his way back to the driver seat. There he waits for her return.

All is calm and clear in the Scenic Mountain Gondola Station. From a staircase surrounded in swirling foggy mists, Audra emerges, breathing in the freshness of the air. The moisture soothes her skin, and a tiny breeze tousles the tulip on her hat. Her lips relax from their tight, default position into a subtle, sealed-lip smile. And for a small moment, she stands there enjoying the peace. Her heart is calm, and her breath is deep, her smile spreads, and then…

The silence breaks. Clacking footsteps echo up from the stairs and throughout the station canopy. Audra jerks from her trance and scurries to her left where she hides behind a nearby pillar. Slowly, she shifts around to discover a mohawked teenager leaning against the cold steel surface of that same pillar. He looks over.

Her eyes go wide. She turns quickly and bolts as fast as she can toward the gondolas, across the station, past the few people trickling into the station. She keeps her head down in hopes that no one will notice, but her clanking cart draws the attention of the passersby. They watch her for a moment, look at each other, and shrug.

While ducking inside the first gondola, Audra steps on the hand of the little lady who was cleaning the floor on her hands and knees. The lady yelps. Flush with embarrassment, Audra squeaks out a "sorry" and rushes away toward another gondola.

Peeking into the second gondola and finding it empty, Audra enters. But the moment she sits, a 10-year-old boy leaps in through the door. "Beat ya," he shouts back to his friend who is running up behind him. They both plop down beside Audra. Her face flushes. Her brow sweats. She promptly leaves.

Quickly, she races to the third gondola, tosses her book cart inside, and grabs the gondola door with both hands. The door squeaks and trembles as she exerts all her strength to pull the door closed.

Breathing heavily, she wipes her sweat with a lace handkerchief and walks toward her book cart. Spotting a bit of grime on the bench, she uses her hankie to clean the spot, which refuses to come off. These things are always so dirty, and it's hard to tell who or what sat here last. She delicately lays the hankie there and sits upon it, while simultaneously selecting the new, green book from her cart. Shifting about to get comfortable, she opens to her bookmark in the middle of the book and relaxes into that trance-like space where the story springs to life in her imagination.

Autumn leaves fly out in all directions. A hooded figure bursts through the bushes, swings from the trees, leaps over a river. She turns around and pulls off her hood, listening. (Besides the tiara, dress, and a different hairstyle, she looks just like Audra.)

Several men rush through the trees behind her. Their

voices echo through the forest. She catches a glimpse of one of them through a tiny clearing in the distant trees. He calls out, "Princess! Come on, now! No need to hide."

The Princess winces in disgust and bounds back to full sprint. Over a log, around a large boulder, up a small hill, she leaps out of the trees onto a dirt road, where large bunches of grass grow in a line down the middle. She looks behind her to see if she has outrun the chasers.

A large, chiseled man, with leather and metal armor, rides up on the back of a majestic unicorn. Startled, the princess whips around and staggers backward, ready to run. "Princess Genevieve," he calls down to her. She pauses, and stares at him for a moment, intrigued by his familiar voice. He hops down from the saddle and reaches out with his strong massive hand and pulls back his hat to reveal his deep, brown eyes.

"Do I know you?" Genevieve asks.

The knightly man smiles and opens his mouth to speak, "ARRRREEEEEEEEEEEEERRREEEEEKKK."

What is that screeching sound? Audra glances up from her book to see the gondola engineer forcing the squeaky door open. He motions with his hand to a group of eager people. As they crowd into the gondola, Audra's shoulders tense up. Of course, she can't always expect to be alone, but she would prefer to travel up the mountain without company. As the crowd grows tighter, she presses her back up closer to the wall. With sideways glances, she searches around for a possible escape route, but there is no way out of her cramped predicament. She notices most of the surrounding people turn their backs to her. As the last gentleman enters, sniffs and turns away, Audra relaxes and buries her face back into the book.

"We met once, as children," the knightly fellow replies.

The chasers' voices come nearer. Genevieve-Audra looks back to the forest in concern.

"Fear not, Princess," the fellow says, "I will never let them find you. Come."

Genevieve hesitates only until the chasers burst into full view. Then she quickly grabs the saddle and pulls herself atop the horse. The Knight hops on in front of her and spurs the horse. Dust fills the air as the horse bolts forward.

Tossed about in the saddle, Genevieve wraps her arms around the rider and looks back to her chasers. In their sprint to follow the stride of the steed, one person trips and the others topple over him. The princess grins triumphantly and looks up at her hero with a slight furrow in her brow.

"So are you going to tell me how I know you? And your name, please?"

Wind tousles the man's full flowing hair as he turns his head in her direction to reply, "WAAAAAAAAAAAAAAA!!!!!"

A baby's cry pulls Audra from her book, once again. She sets the book down and slowly stands to peek through the crowd. One mother is holding a smiling baby, gently bouncing and kissing her little one. The crying baby's mother, in contrast, stands completely still, fixated on a fashion magazine. Audra squints her eyes and shakes her head in disapproval. Mothers these days ... so distracted. Audra plops back down on the bench.

"WAAAAAAAAAAAAAAA!!!!" the baby continues.

"Shhhhhhh," hisses a grumpy old man in a patched-up old jacket.

Audra fidgets nervously, her eyes darting. At first, she passively wishes the baby would stop. Then she spots a binky near the heel of the mother's red shoe. Audra looks from her book to the binky to her book. She decides to dive back into the book, but the baby's volume increases.

"WAAAAAAAAAAAAAAAAAAAAAA!!!"

Audra scowls and drops her book back to the cart. With both hands holding to the bench, she lowers herself down and reaches for the binky with her right foot, trying hard not to bump any of the surrounding standers. The binky is too far away, so she holds on with one hand and lengthens her body sideways, lower to the ground. Her pointy shoe touches the binky, but a hefty gentleman shifts his weight, bumps her leg, and knocks the binky further away. She reaches again and brushes against the leg of the old patched-up-jacket man. He glares down.

Audra scrambles back to her seat, her face flushed red, and stares down at the ground until the man looks away. The baby continues to cry, but Audra shrinks down and plugs her ears. Sadly, to retrieve her book she has to unplug one ear, but she snatches it quickly. With her elbows, she holds the book open on her lap, not realizing she has skipped a page. She continues to read:

Genevieve-Audra leaps from the horse and runs up the tower stairs. The prince watches her from his unicorn. His smile fades to sadness. As she reaches the top of the stairs, Genevieve lets out a giddy laugh and she scans her surroundings. At the sound of the galloping horse, she runs to the window, catching only a glimpse of her hero riding away.

"Goodbye, Prince Ruben," she says to the afternoon air. And to her new living quarters, "Hello solitude."

“Hmm,” Audra smiles as she lovingly shuts her novel. She whispers, “Hello solitude.” She would give anything to be permanently alone.

The gondola stops. The baby still wails. As the passengers shuffle out, their feet kick the binky around the floor. Audra spots it. Her eyes follow it back and forth until it slides out into the open. She swiftly snatches it up then tosses it over the crowd.

The binky hits the top of the gossip magazine and bounces away into the dirt. The mother finally looks up at her cranky baby. “Why won’t you just be quiet,” the mother whines as she follows the others. The binky remains, covered in filth.

Audra gathers her items and waits just inside the gondola door, spying on the others as they walk away. The forest is much more pleasant when she can walk alone, without a person in sight. She has learned to be patient, to wait until she is entirely alone. As the doors slide closed, Audra scrambles out.

She continues to watch the others from behind a nearby tree. Most of them follow the path to the right. As the gondola glides down and away, Audra hurries down the less-traveled route to the left. She can still hear voices chattering in the distance, but at least she feels somewhat alone.

On the side of the mountain, in a grove of aspen trees, she pulls the picnic blanket from her cart basket. She flips it in the air and lets it settle across the ground. She sits down and spreads out her goodies: a pesto mozzarella sandwich, kiwi salad, chocolate éclairs, and finally her array of books. She admires her feast. Her lips spread into a full smile. But this smile quickly fades as she turns to the last item the picnic basket.

She retrieves a pair of binoculars and holds them with both hands, which start to tremble as if they are holding hot coals. She stares at the binoculars for a long moment. Her heart rate increases, her breathing grows faster, and she bites her lower lip and lifts them to her eyes.

Chapter 2: A New Home.

Tightly-gripped, the binoculars press red rings into her face. She scans the mountainside across the valley, down, over, criss-cross, until she finds a cabin there. With the flip of a switch, the cabin detail magnifies.

It's a nice, quaint little place, embellished by flowers and well-maintained. Audra can't help but fantasize herself living there. From an imaginary puff of orange-yellow smoke, she daydreams an Imaginary-Audra materializing on the cabin porch. Real-Audra delights as she watches her imaginary self spread out on the lounging chair.

With a pleasant smile, Real-Audra takes a

moment away from the binoculars to reach inside the cover of her Circus Elephant book. She pulls out a folded sheet of paper along with an envelope from the United International Bank. She unfolds the paper to review the many photos of homes glued in perfect rows. Each house has a big red X drawn through it, except this cabin at the end of the list.

Again through the binoculars, she imagines herself in the garden spraying plant food on the daisies, in her kitchen sipping hot cider, on the roof staring into the sky.

With dreamy eyes and a blissful smile, Real-Audra slowly drops the binoculars from her eyes and breathes a deep, joyful breath. It seems that though it's the last, this cabin could still be the one!

"Thank you," she whispers to the heavens.

Suddenly, a distant, joyful shout reaches her ears. She whips the binoculars up again and scans out across the valley, right to the spot where her imaginary self still sunbathes on the roof. A real figure zips past on a zip line. Imaginary-Audra sits up, startled, and bursts back into orange-yellow smoke.

Following the zip line twenty feet up the mountain, Real-Audra spots another cabin, partially hidden by trees. There she sees several real people in their swimsuits, enjoying a high-energy party filled with laughter, colorful drinks, and pranksters. One strapping fellow swings down from the roof and pushes a couple into the pool on his sprint toward the zip line. He jumps and grips the zip line handles. Real-Audra's binoculars follow him down until he passes her dream cabin, where Imaginary-Audra materializes again on the lounging chair.

Two imaginary zip-liners, made of blue-green smoke, pummel her with water balloons as they pass. Imaginary-Audra jumps up from her chair and rushes into the front door. A group of wild imaginary partiers run up her front stairs and pound on the door. One of them spots her through the window and jumps in through the glass. He opens the front door, letting the others enter. They chase the screaming Imaginary-Audra throughout the house, opening and slamming doors, emptying her cabinets, knocking over furniture, until they are all hanging out the windows, teasing Imaginary-Audra as she climbs out a window and up a ladder, toward the roof. Suddenly, she slips and plummets to the ground. At the moment of impact, she and all the imaginary others burst into smoke. Only an empty, deserted cabin remains.

Real-Audra lowers her binoculars with a disappointed scowl. She rubs her forehead with her right hand as she tosses the binoculars away with her left. Groaning, she lays down on her side and stares at her list of red-x homes.

With a thick red marker, she crosses out the mountain-side cabin, the last home on the list. She smashes the list down into the basket, and sighs. So much for that fantasy.

Her only option left rests inside this unopened envelope from the Unified International Bank. Shifting her legs, she turns the envelope over and slides her fingers in. But before she can rip it even an inch, a pain surges up from her foot causing her whole body to jolt. She tosses the letter aside and looks at that foot.

A furry honeybee scrambles out from under her heel, leaving its stinger embedded in the middle of a red spot on Audra's foot. She bites her lip and winces. Serves her right for stepping on the poor creature. With her long fingernails, she carefully clamps down below the stinger's venom bag, pulls it out, and rubs the pain away.

She reaches back for the partially-opened envelope just as another honeybee lands on it. Lifting the letter, she gently scoops the bee into the palm of her hand and releases it into the air, all without getting stung. She places her finger back under the flap, in preparation to open the rest of the seal, but because of a nervous pulse in the pit of her stomach, she stops, shakes her head, and stores the envelope and her list of red-x homes in the back cover of her Circus Elephant book.

In a rush, she puts away the food, picnic blanket, and books. She limps back down the path towards the gondola, pulling her cart over the bumps and around the clumps of trail-grass. When the gondola comes into view, Audra slows her pace. She carefully approaches, opens the door, looks around at the emptiness, and heads right for the bench. Audra closes her eyes and breathes deeply. Her body continues to fidget with nervous energy, and she sighs three times before reaching for the newest book from her cart. Reading could cheer her up.

She opens to Chapter 3 and smooths its bright-white pages. She reads:

Lightning cracks. Rain pours. The waves rock the ship as Bonny O'Malley tiptoes through a crowd of sleeping, smelly shipmates. (Bonny looks just like Audra, in pirate clothing). With a knapsack over her shoulder, she hurries up the stairs, and out onto the rain-soaked deck. She scurries toward the ropes securing the lifeboats and unties one of the knots.

Loud footsteps pound toward her as a grizzled voice seethes, "No one leaves my ship." She jumps up onto the railing, lets go of the rope and leaps toward the sinking lifeboat just as the captain's meaty arm reaches out to grab her. He barely misses her knapsack.

"Naarrrg," He yells as she falls away from his grasp.

Water splashes in all directions as the lifeboat hits against the ocean. Audra-Bonny looks back up at the Captain, who has lashed a rope around his waist and is preparing to jump in after her. Suddenly, a flying saucer appears in the sky above him, blocking out the rain and sending flashes of light in all directions. Both Audra-Bonny and the captain gasp as they turn toward the alien spaceship.

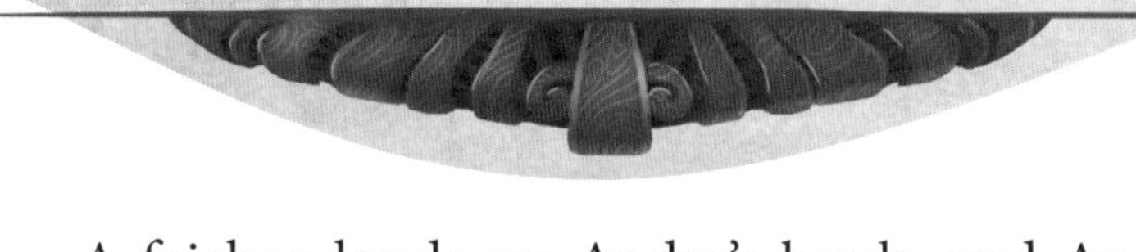

A frisbee lands on Audra's book, and Audra looks up, startled.

"Oh yeah!" shouts a familiar 10-year-old boy as he skips toward the gondola, "got it in!" His friends follow after him, laughing. As he enters, he looks sheepishly at Audra for a moment, opening his mouth perhaps to apologize, but he is distracted by a slap on the back from his friend.

Straight-faced and disturbed, Audra tosses the frisbee aside and darts to the opposite end of the gondola. The boys gather in a circle on their end, whispering and giggling, pointing every so often at Audra and laughing some more. Though she tries to keep a straight face, her jaw clenches, and her eyes grow sad. "Kids these days," she mutters under her breath.

She stores her book away in her cart and turns to stare out the window. Someone sits beside her, and a tiny little hand pats her on the arm. Audra turns slowly to see the baby from earlier, who is now cheerful in contrast to his mother, who appears quite exhausted.

Audra can't help but smile at the beautiful child. The baby smiles back. She gives him a little wave. The baby reaches out to her. She shifts, nervously.

"He wants you to hold him," The mother says with a faint smile.

"Oh no," Audra pulls away with a smile. "I shouldn't." With her luck, the baby would probably cry if she did.

She turns back to the window. The entire ride down the mountain, she continues staring out, longing for the solitude she may never find.

As they reach the base, she bolts through the door.

She hurries back through the station, down the stairs, and toward her limo. She pulls her hat down at a diagonal and passes Norman, with no eye contact. She slips into the vehicle. Norman shuts the door.

On the limo seat next to Audra, the rose from Norman waits. She picks it up, smells it, and gradually, she smiles. Norman is a fine gentleman in her mind. She doesn't know how to react when he stares at her and grins. She smells the rose again, glancing up at Norman's reflection in the rear-view mirror. His handsome eyes remain focused, steering the limo into the sunset. Audra looks again at the rose and then back at Norman. His gaze meets hers. She looks away, smells the rose once more, and finally places it back on the seat. Romantic relationships, at this point, are out of the question.

After passing some farms, skyscrapers, and a bunch of glitzy homes, the limo stops in front of an elegant townhome in the middle of the bustling city. In contrast to the cold rigidness of the urban surroundings, Audra's home is decorated with carved Victorian finishes, bay windows, and plenty of variety and angles to give it character. Norman exits the driver's seat and walks around to Audra's door. She slowly emerges.

Norman swallows and whispers, "Audra?"

Hardly glancing up, she places a note in his hand. His face lights up, and his eyes follow her as she hurries around the large hedges hiding her front door. He opens the letter, his hands shaking slightly, and reads:

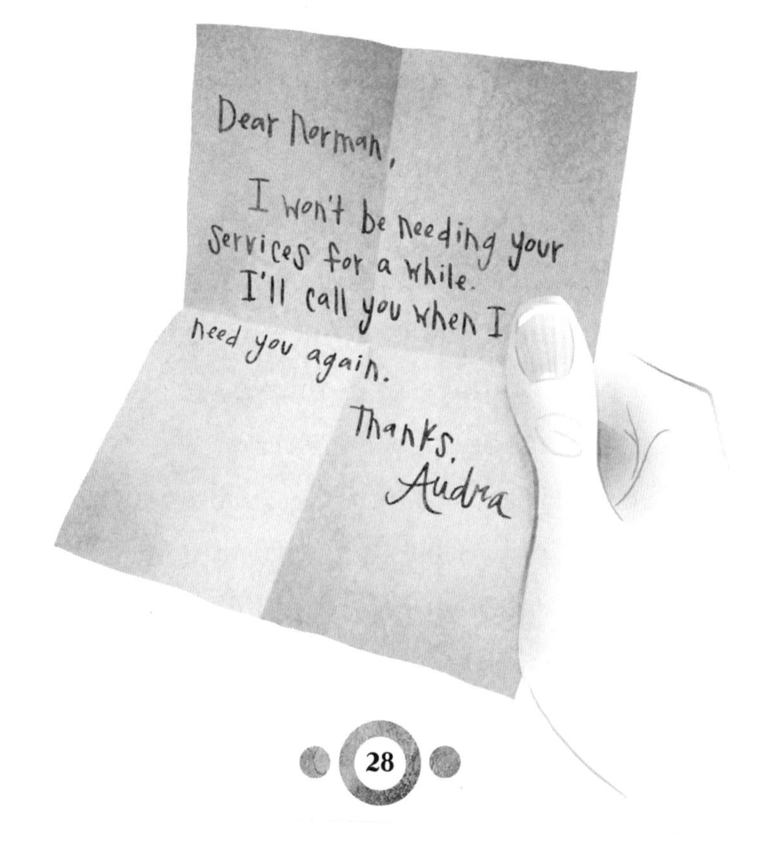
Dear Norman,

I won't be needing your services for a while. I'll call you when I need you again.

Thanks,
Audra

Norman hangs his head, pockets the note and heads to his driver seat. He starts the limousine and drives away slowly, pausing a long time before turning the corner.

Audra sighs as she watches him drive away. He's such a nice man, but Audra could never give him the attention and companionship he needs. She turns toward her house, approaches her doorway, slowly pulls out her keychain, inserts the key, sighs again, and turns the key.

The sound of a snapping branch alerts her. She whips around to see a spinning softball, speeding through the air toward her face.

Chapter 3: Three Grown Sisters

In an ultra-fast reflex, Audra's hand whips up and catches the ball.

It stops a half-inch from the tip of her nose.

"Good evening, Kendra," she says, straight-faced.

Kendra—a grown woman, dressed like a teenage boy—struts out of the shadows, clapping her hands and chuckling to herself. "I keep telling you, sis, you could be a powerhouse if you'd just come to the gym with me." She puts her meaty hands around Audra's arm. "We've got to get some muscle on those skinny bones."

Some people might smile and brush off this type of teasing, but not Audra. Her brows scrunch

down in anger. She quickly turns and walks in through her front door. Kendra follows. Audra sets her keys on the table in the entryway and touches the framed picture surrounded by flowers. Her mother and father were lovely people, inside and out. Now all she had left of her parents were photographs and memories. She gives them an affectionate nod hello and heads toward her circular staircase.

Vast stretches of built-in bookshelves line every wall in her home, with tons of books stashed in various spaces upstairs.

Kendra stays behind and stares at the framed memorial. "Oh mama," she says, "I never will know why Audra was your favorite."

Audra climbs the staircase to see her other sister Natalia, glamorous as a supermodel, draped across the couch while watching the television. Kendra's voice floats up from downstairs. "Can you believe mom's been gone for a whole year now?"

Audra quietly sits down on the edge of the couch and looks at the television to see beautifully dressed acrobats swinging from silks in a dazzling circus.

"Hello, Natalia," Audra says timidly, glancing over.

Natalia's eyes remain fixated on the television. "Ahh, look at that glitz and glam. Isn't it beautiful?"

"Sure," says Audra. "A little wild for my taste."

"After this program ends, you should come with me to the spa," says Natalia, her eyes still on the television. "You are obviously overdue for a makeover."

Audra lets out a sigh with a thick, tired groan. Natalia hasn't even looked at her once, yet she always recommends a makeover no matter how Audra tries.

"What's she doing here?" Kendra grumbles, stomping up the last few stairs.

Natalia finally breaks her gaze from the TV and snaps toward Kendra, "I come here all the time."

"Really?" asks Kendra, irritated. "every minute of every day?"

"Every minute you aren't hogging the air" Natalia stands.

"I invited you both," Audra quietly interjects,

then mutters under her breath, "even though it terrified me."

"Alright pipsqueak," Kendra says in a hostile tone, rolling her eyes toward Audra, "What is this about?" Her tone quickly changes to sarcasm, "Mother's money, I hope. I've never felt so poor."

Natalia cuts in, "Why? Still throwing it away on horse races and fitness fads?"

"At least I'm not wasting it on makeovers and ridiculous fashion statements," Kendra shouts into Natalia's face.

Audra stands and interjects, "The reason I invited you both—"

"Be quiet," Kendra shouts, shoving Audra, who falls to a sitting position against the couch.

"Don't treat her that way!" shouts Natalia.

"Oh," says Kendra in a devious voice, "you don't want to open that can of sardines."

"What sardines?"

"I'm sure you don't want me to tell Audra about the lawyer you hired because you feel she is unfit to execute mother's will. Or about how you and your fashionistas laugh about the way she dresses."

"Please," Audra says a little louder, sitting a little straighter on the couch.

"QUIET!" both sisters shout.

Audra slumps back against the pillows and watches the television while her sisters carry on, fighting just for the sake of fighting. Sadly, she should have known it would go this way, but she has never made this big of a decision on her own. She always had her mother for advice.

"Just like when we were kids," Natalia shouts, "you never change!"

Audra muses to herself, whispering, "Obviously none of us do."

The television program on dazzling acrobats has now shifted its cameras to clowns.

Natalia and Kendra continue fighting, getting louder and less-intelligent by the second. Audra looks from the television to Kendra, who grabs a decorative ball from the table and paces while tossing it. Audra looks back to the TV as the clowns are juggling. Audra's left eyebrow raises in amusement. She turns to Natalia, whose pretty face is contorting in all sorts of angry expressions, crazy faces, just like the clowns as they show off their craziest walks. Audra's sisters stomp around the home, mad with anger for each other. The clowns kick each other in their posteriors while Natalia dodges Kendra's kick. Audra chuckles. But the amusement ends when Kendra throws the decorative ball at Natalia, who ducks.

The ball breaks a mirror. Startled, Audra jumps up.

Natalia throws her hands in the air, "That's it. I'm out of here." She stomps out of the room and down the circular, grand staircase.

"Ah no!" Kendra growls, following her like a vulture. "We're taking this outside!"

"If you so much as touch me, I'll sue!"

"Wait," Audra chases them both in a panic, "I haven't told you, yet. It's important." The door comes into Audra's view as Kendra and Natalia are storming out.

Audra shouts out after them, "I just wanted you to know—"

SLAM.

Audra lets out a hefty sigh, hangs her head, slumps her shoulders, and finishes her sentence, "—that I'm leaving civilization for a while. Not that you care."

She looks again at her memorial to her parents. "Oh mamma, I wish you were here. You'd tell me not to do this. 'It's too foolish,' you'd say."

Audra trudges up the stairs toward her couch. "But what else can I do?" She flops down in front of the television, lays her head back on the cushions, and shuts her eyes. The music from the circus program shifts to a more serious tone. At the sound of an elephant groaning in pain, Audra opens her eyes and leans toward the television.

"But the circus isn't always glamorous behind the scenes," says a female voice on the television, "For some circus animals, it can even be tragic." The featured elephant struggles under ropes as its trainer pokes it with a training stick, forcing the poor beast to balance on its hind legs. Next, the trainers force the elephant to keep its hindquarters in the air while they force its head and frontal legs into a bow.

Audra shuts the television off, revealing her reflection staring back at her with a forlorn face, tears rolling down her cheeks, holding the remote control in her trembling hand.

She stands up and paces about the floor, messing up her hair with her fidgety fingers. "Why are people so terrible?" The frustration boils up inside of her, searching for an escape. She picks up a pillow and screams into it.

"Aaaaaahhhhh!"

When her scream runs out, she drops the pillow while hurrying toward the double doors that lead to her porch garden. Pulling both doors open, she rushes out and grabs onto the bars of the overhanging garden trellis.

The view of the skyscrapers, through the vertical white bars of the trellis, makes Audra look and feel like a double-caged prisoner. And inside her heart, that is just how Audra feels.

She must do something. She must end this pain. It's time to put her plan into action.

"I know what you're thinking," says the voice of an imaginary, 5-inch-tall version of Natalia who materializes from a puff of red smoke on Audra's shoulder, "But you are not an elephant. And this is not a cage." Audra glances sideways at her transparent sister.

"Don't listen to her," says Imaginary-Kendra, who materializes from a puff of red smoke on Audra's other shoulder. "You only need to beef up a bit. Then you can be any kind of elephant you want." Kendra bursts out laughing, obviously pleased with her clever insult.

Audra looks back and forth at her imaginary sisters, both transparent, both 5 inches tall, both wearing red. Kendra still dresses like a teenage boy and Natalia still looks like she walked off a fashion show runway.

"It's official," Audra says to herself, walking back

inside while her sisters ride on her shoulders, "I've lost my mind."

"That's what I was going to say," Imaginary-Natalia says, blow drying her voluminous hair. Audra pulls out the unopened envelope and the list of red-x'd homes from her *Circus Elephant* book. She throws the list away and stares at the envelope, genuinely nervous.

"You want to waist a third of your inheritance on that?" Imaginary-Natalia grumbles.

"Don't listen to her!" shouts Imaginary-Kendra while swinging from the loose end of Audra's scarf, "I'm all for it. It'll build character, make you stronger." With that, she lets go and vaults into the air, bursting into a puff of red smoke.

"Whatever," Imaginary-Natalia says, slowly fading away as her red smoke spins away from Audra's shoulder, "Do what you want. And if you don't come back, we'll gladly take care of the rest of your inheritance." With that, she completely vanishes.

Audra kisses the envelope for good luck, places it back in the cover of *The Circus Elephant*, and springs into action. She pulls several books off her shelf, tossing them into the suitcase on her bed: When she picks up *Peter Pan*, she can almost feel the wind as Wendy and boys follow Peter toward the second star on the right. With *Lord of the Flies*, Audra can hear the boys chasing each other with spears through the flaming forest. With *Moby Dick*, she can smell the fishy mist rising from the ocean. And with *Robinson Crusoe*, she can feel the breeze on the deck of a ship sailing the open sea.

After the fictional books, she throws in a medical textbook, clothes, and shoes. To top off the suitcase, she places *The Circus Elephant* book inside and slips a picture of her parents in the front cover. She zips up the suitcase and sighs with satisfaction.

A door slams downstairs as Real-Kendra returns through the front door. "I'm sleeping on the couch tonight," she shouts up to Audra. She runs up the stairs and leaps onto the couch, switching on a football game at full volume.

Audra comes in with a blanket for Kendra. "So that you know, I'll be away for a while. The security system will set once you leave tomorrow."

"Okay, great, whatever," Kendra says in a careless tone.

Audra tries to clarify. "That means you won't be able to get in for a long time."

"Keep it down, will ya? I'm trying to watch the game!"

Audra shuts herself in her room and opens her laptop, pulling up a web-browser with many pre-selected tabs. In the first website for Christian Howard's Helicopters, she points to the purchase button and lifts her finger to click, but her finger wavers above the button. Her breathing becomes rapid. She starts to pull her finger away. Was she going to do this? What would Mamma say?

"Come on," says a puff of swirling smoke, which sounds like Kendra, passing her ear. "Are you a weakling or what?"

Click!

Momma would agree that Audra was a grown woman. She could make her own choices.

Audra moves to the next website for new home furnishings, clicks ORDER, then to the next and click, to the next. Click, click, click!

She takes a deep breath before pressing the confirm button to wire three million dollars to the Unified National Bank. She had saved the most challenging click for last, hoping that by the time she'd reached it, her nerves would be numb. And as she expected, she now feels fully committed. She clicks and exhales in relief.

It's finally finished. She's finally going to get away. She gently closes her laptop and strides across the room to her closet door.

From a ribbon-wound hanger, she retrieves her fluffy nightgown and changes her clothes behind the dressing screen. Her gown shimmers as she enters the moonlight sifting in through her large bay window. The gentle breeze tousles her nightgown.

Light from an apartment across the street catches her eye. A man stands, staring down at her through his telescope. She shuts the curtains in disgust. "Go to bed, Bill," she mumbles. She strolls toward her bed.

The moment she lays down, party music comes roaring from the house next door. Audra marches past the curtains, looks out at the partiers in disgust, and slams the window shut.

As neighbors often do, they turn the music up louder.

Between the loud party racket, the football game in the other room, and Kendra yelling as if the players could hear her, the whole house reverberates with noise.

With a groan, Audra picks up one of her medical books and flips on the light beside her bed. Concentration is impossible. She slams her book down and pulls a pillow over her head.

A restless night follows.

Chapter 4: The Big White Box

The sun rises on the city, peeking where it can through the skyscrapers and freeways. One patch of light streaks across Audra's front lawn, reflecting off the surface of an enormous, white box sitting in the center of the grass.

An athletic woman in a jogging suit and headphones runs behind her dog on the sidewalk. When they pass the big white box, the dog barks across the lawn towards it. The woman keeps on running, the leash tightens, and she drags the scrambling dog behind her.

From behind some bushes in the front yard, Audra cheerfully lugs her suitcase and box toward the big white box. She types a code on the pin-pad on the side. Gears and switches clank from inside. The door pops open. With all the strength she can muster, Audra pulls the door open oh-so-slowly. She slips in with her suitcase and straining, grunting, groaning, she gradually pulls the door shut.

A couple of cars zoom past.

A robin lands on the corner of the big white box.

Little else happens for the next several minutes. Cars continue driving by. A few pedestrians pass on both sides of the street.

A limousine drives up and out steps Norman, rehearsing a speech: "I know you say you don't need me, Audra, but I don't think it's good for you to keep locking yourself in your house for weeks on end. Your sisters always show up, make a stink, and you–"

Norman stops and stares at the big white box, tilting his head in a puzzled expression.

A strong gust of wind nearly knocks Norman over as a helicopter descends from above. It rustles

the trees, blowing leaves and petals all around Audra's yard.

Kendra stumbles out of the front door in her bathrobe. "What's the ruckus?"

Natalia pulls up in her convertible and holds onto her hair to prevent its whipping about in the wind.

Together, they watch as the helicopter lifts into the air and pulls the white box up with a cable.

Natalia is the first to break her trance, "Where's Audra?"

Kendra yawns and heads back toward the front door. "She's not inside. I heard her leave this morning."

Natalia looks at Norman.

"And she's not in the limo, so–" Norman stops.

"Noooo!" Kendra shrieks, stumbling away from the front door, "What? It's locked?"

"Audra!" Norman shouts, running in the direction of the helicopter, which was no bigger than a speck against the clouds.

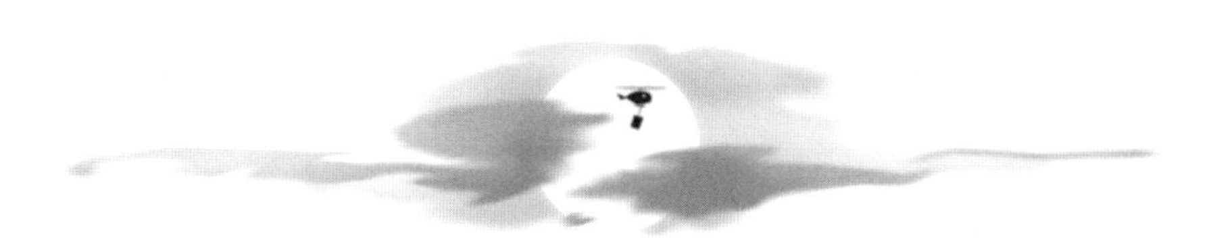

Inside the big white box, bookshelves line the walls. Pristine, unread books line the shelves. Decorative curtains lend the room a cozy feel. A large, ornate mirror hangs on the back wall behind Audra.

There she sits on a fluffy couch, holding a package wrapped in brown paper. Before opening the box, she removes the unopened envelope from the cover of *The Circus Elephant* book and rips it open. She beams with pride at the contents: a picture of a private island for sale, along with it she finds an inspection sheet stamped with a unique red logo featuring a crawdad — the verdict of the report: uninhabited.

She lets out a giddy squeal. "And now it's all mine," she whispers.

She then rips the brown paper off the wrapped package and finds a framed deed of ownership along with another picture of the island, this one also framed.

Her smile couldn't grow any more full. Not

many people can say they own a private island. And she, Audra Jones, is thrilled to be one of them.

She sets her new treasures aside and settles into the couch. With one arm, she leans on the table while she reads her well-worn copy of *The Circus Elephant*. With the other arm, Audra absent-mindedly eats her peanut-butter-and-jelly sandwich. She reads intently, envisioning the scene of Elphie and Chimpy's tea party. Chimpy's monkey friends pop over to the tea party and Elphie trembles so nervously her lips can barely take a sip. One monkey pops up behind her, and she jumps into the air, tossing tea all over Chimpy. Audra, the monkeys, and Chimpy laugh pleasantly together. Elphie is not amused.

Suddenly, the whole white box jolts, having been dropped onto a hard surface. The imaginary scene of Elphie and Chimpy dissolves into a puff of smoke. Audra and all the contents bounce up into the air. The peanut butter and jam sandwich smears across Audra's face. A few books from one of the shelves fall around her. She jumps up on the couch and stops the remainder of the books from falling off the shelves.

From the big white box's angled resting position on the metal ramp, it slides downward, gaining momentum toward a massive ship in the port by the sea. A group of women panic and chase the box down the ramp. They shout a warning to a group of men at the bottom of the incline. One of the chasers reaches the chain and tries with all her might to reverse the box's downward slide. More join her in pulling the cable as the group from below runs up to help. After many grunts, groans, and veins bulging out of their foreheads, the team successfully eases the big white box onto the ship deck.

They all shake out their arms and wipe the sweat from their faces. "Good job team," one of the women says. "Tragedy avoided!"

Inside the box, Audra digs out from beneath a pile of books. She climbs out on top and staggers about, dizzy. When she looks into the cracked mirror, several wild-haired-Audras stare back at her with peanut butter and jelly smeared across their faces.

Audra chuckles and pulls a lace handkerchief

from her pocket to wipe her face clean. She then smoothes her hair until it is perfect.

Book by book, she restocks the shelves of the white box.

Outside, the workers carefully put the big white box into a safe place surrounded by the wooden crates on the ship deck.

Inside, Audra admires her completely restocked shelves and sits down on her comfy couch with an unusual squish. She stands up, turns around, and peels her peanut butter and jelly sandwich from the back of her skirt. She grumbles.

After the ship pulls out of the harbor, the rest of the trip is somewhat repetitive.

As the boat rocks, the books fall off their shelves again. Audra patiently puts them all back. Later during naptime, the books fall once more, but this time Audra doesn't put them back. She pulls out her fluffy couch cushions and naps on top of the book pile. After that, she reads and eats once more.

The ship continues out into the ocean. As the sun sets behind the ship, another helicopter flies over and retrieves the big white box. It carries

Audra far into the distance and sets her down on the shore of a sandy, white beach.

Four other helicopters bring in a house and lower it down on the stilts at the uphill side of the beach. Construction women and men work all night putting finishing touches on the pre-built house and walkway, unpacking boxes, and double checking the solar panels on the roof.

As the workers climb into the helicopters and fly away from the island, the sky lights up with a golden sunrise.

The big white box waits alone on the sand.

Chapter 5: Paradise

An ocean wave crawls up the sandy beach and touches the corner of the big white box, leaving a bit of sea foam wherever it touches. The water rolls down while another wave comes in. A small crab pops out from under the box, followed by a couple of baby crabs. A single seagull swoops down to harass the little ones. The momma crab snaps at the seagull, viciously defending her babies.

Twisting gears and clicking bolts sound from within the walls of the white box. The door inches open. Audra peeks out and slowly pushes the door outward, emerging from the base like a snail from its shell. She looks around the island, shoulders tense, eyes wide.

At sight of her new beach home, a smile spreads across her face. She scans every inch of the view: the island, the sky, the jungle, all without any sign of other humans. Upon finding herself completely alone, her shoulders relax. Her nerves calm. She tips her head back and breathes the ocean air deep into her lungs. "Mmm. Perfect."

Leaving her shoes behind, she leaps out like a jack-in-the-box onto the empty beach, skipping and running like she hasn't felt comfortable to do since she was a 4-year-old child. She shouts joyfully, as loud as her lungs can handle. She kicks sand in the air with her bare feet, does cartwheels down to the ocean, and splashes around in the ocean waves, cheering and laughing some more. She releases her hair. It falls on her shoulders. Her feet sink into the sand, and tiny crabs pop out between her toes.

She strolls up to the ramp leading up to her house and admires the many windows. She saunters in through the door and grabs a banana from the bowl next to a bulky electronic communication device. She picks up what looks like half of an old-fashioned telephone, with swirls in its cord. She presses the red button.

"Testing. Testing. This is Ivory801."

She waits and listens a moment.

"Loud and clear," says a female voice from the device speaker. "Let us know when you need supplies, and we'll airdrop them to you!"

Audra turns back to her empty home and sighs in satisfaction. "Perfect," she says.

She wanders around her apartment, admiring the features of her new beach home: a lovely couch, aged-wood window seats, and an ornate white kitchen table with four padded chairs. She runs her hand along a large bookshelf. It covers only one wall, but the books are stacked two layers deep. And at the end of the one-room home, she hops up on the cushy circular bed, steps through the pillows and opens the curtains surrounding her sleeping area. And there through the large windows, she enjoys the vast ocean view.

"All alone on a beautiful island," Audra shouts

as she runs out down the ramp and out onto the open beach. “Finally! Solitude!” She dives into the ocean waves, snatches seashells from the water and inspects them. Some, she slips in her pocket. Others, she throws back to the sea. She plays like this for hours, further down the beach and away from her comfortable new home, until she looks back and realizes she can’t even see her home. Her journey has curved away, and trees now block her view.

She decides to saunter back to her new home, but on her first step in that direction, her foot touches something unusual.

Looking down, she discovers a glass bottle. She retrieves the bottle and inspects it. It has a matte texture as if it has spent years rolling in the sand, losing its shine. When held up in the setting sun, the glass distorts her view of the bright colored reflections on the ocean. And in that distorted view, near one of the distant mini-islands, she spots something triangular, red with a splotch of white, moving across the water at a rapid speed.

She must be seeing things.

Audra lowers the bottle and inspects it from

a different angle, scratching at it to see if maybe something in the bottle itself was tricking her eyes. She looks back up and scans the mini islands looking for that strange triangular shape, but there is no sign of anything unnatural. So she shrugs it off. "Yep, seeing things."

Unexpected stormclouds brew above the trees, reflecting some of the sunset colors to contrast their deep, dark tones. What a gloomy ending to Audra's perfect arrival day. But was it perfect? What about the triangular shape with the splotch of red? Had it been a trick of her eye?

One last time, she scans the ocean near the mini island, and seeing nothing but sea, land, and sky, she turns to run along the forest edge. Twenty feet forward and she spots a piece of fabric snagged on a sharp branch. She stops and examines the material with its bold pattern of bright orange and blues.

She pockets the fabric, continues her run while shaking her head. That fabric could have come from anywhere. It could have washed up on shore and blown up into the clutches of the branch. It could have ... but that would be far fetched.

Rain sprinkles at first, and then it falls, and then it pours. Audra shields her eyes and watches the ground while continuing her run. But after several minutes of running, she wonders if she should have arrived by now.

She stops and checks her surroundings, and when she spots her home, she gasps.

Her new home has been completely covered with fallen trees, palm leaves, vines, and vegetation of all sorts.

Imaginary-Natalia puffs out on Audra's shoulder. "Look, the forest is eating your home." She bursts out laughing, pleased with her joke.

Audra is not pleased at all.

Imaginary-Kenda joins them. "Natalia, this is serious. Her home's already eaten!"

The sisters roll with laughter on Audra's shoulders.

Audra completely ignores them, entranced by the wondrous sight and the scent of greenery in the rain. Confusion twitches through every feature of Audra's face.

"Come on Audra," says Imaginary-Natalia, recovering from her fit of laughter. "Don't spoil a good joke. Laugh with us." Both shoulder sisters stare up at Audra.

Holding onto her skirt, Audra tiptoes through the obstacle course leading up the ramp to her door. Her imaginary sisters ride on her shoulders until about halfway up the incline and then fade away in boredom. At the top of the ramp, Audra takes a deep breath and holds it.

Chapter 6: The Forest's Welcome

The rain pours from massive storm clouds, which now extend past the horizon. Lightning flashes above the ocean, so far in the distance that the thunder comes in as a low rumble, as soft as a hum.

Pulling back the vines blocking her door, Audra quickly turns the knob, enters and flips on the light. Once she sees the room appears to be empty, she finally starts breathing. Audra quickly darts around, checking behind the furniture. With her arms extended and trembling, she approaches the closet, summoning all her courage to check behind the double doors.

She closes her eyes and pulls both doors so hard that they swing and hit the walls. She screams and jumps back, startled by the sound. Fortunately, the closet is empty, except a few hanging coats and empty hangers. She holds her chest and takes a deep breath.

"Oh, Audra," she says, relaxing completely, feeling quite silly. She walks out through the empty room toward her kitchen area.

Without warning, a bolt of lightning flashes outside and hits one of the branches on her roof, it surges down the tree branch and completely fries a nearby solar panel. Electric current travels down the wire and into the battery that powers Audra's home. Her lights and power disappear entirely.

Audra groans, standing in the middle of her dark, one-room home. Just her luck, this is her first night here, and the power is completely gone. The only light source she has left is the soft, blue glow coming in through the uncovered windows.

Another lightning flash lights up the window behind her, revealing the silhouette of a man in a top hat and strange clothes, hiding inside the window curtains. But Audra doesn't see it. She only catches a glimpse of fading light and shadow.

She rushes over to the window and looks out at the moonlit rain and wind-blown trees. Again, she doesn't see the strangely dressed man staring out from behind the curtain with his big green eyes. He wears goggles and a top hat, heaps of striped fabric. Several elements of his clothing are reminiscent of a honey bee.

Audra turns and walks away from the window. The mystery man sneaks out to follow her, nervously fiddling with his grey-streaked-black beard.

Lightning flashes again and the man slips into the shadows near Audra just as she whips around again.

"You're a grown woman, Audra," she scolds herself. "Do try to remain calm." But she feels

anything but calm. Her body continues to tremble as she advances toward the sink.

Still unseen by Audra, the strange man smiles and follows her, staying low and timing his steps to the exact moment of Audra's. Clumsy because of the dark, Audra trips on a chair and falls over it. The man reaches out to help, then pulls his hand back and shakes his head.

Audra scrambles to her feet and hurries to the sink. This stress is unbearable, but maybe some tea will calm her hyper heart. She reaches for the teacups hanging beside the moonlit sink. The man takes a few more steps around the table but freezes as he steps on a squeaky board. Lighting and thunder burst together outside. The stranger quickly ducks and hides beneath the table just as Audra turns around. She stares for a moment into the darkness and then hurries back to the table with her teacup, herbal tea bag, and crackers. She sits down and nervously starts to brew her cold cup of tea.

Not paying any attention to the slowly rising top hat beside her, Audra sets her teacup right upon that hat as she stands up to retrieve the sugar bowl from beside the sink. The man in the top hat bites his lip and stays almost perfectly still, except his eyes, which follow Audra around the room.

Audra sits back in her seat and retrieves the cup to stir in some sugar. The hat drifts away toward the sink as the man crawls quickly and silently away. Audra sips her tea for a moment, and then a puzzled expression creeps onto her face.

She looks to the side where the hat had been, then under the table. She looks back to the window where the stranger had initially been hiding. Suddenly her subconscious screams at her: there has been someone hiding and following her around the apartment. Though something in her had sensed it, she only now allowed herself to believe it.

A breeze fills the room as her front door swings open and bangs against the wall. Just as Audra glances over, a flash of lightning lights up the silhouette of the stranger in the doorway. He rushes away into the rainstorm.

Audra leaps over to her communication device, keeping her eyes on the door. She reaches back to grab the receiver, but as her hand grasps at the space where the device once was, all she can find is a banana.

"Help! Emergency," she shouts into the banana, "There's someone here on the..."

She stops and looks at the banana and then to where her device once was. Her eyes fill with shock, "He stole it!"

She runs out in the rain and looks through the rain into the darkness. A distant male voice shouts something she can't quite understand, something like "get out of here" or "looky here." Audra quickly hops back inside, shuts and deadbolts the door, and paces her apartment.

"What? No, I can't. What do I? I didn't. Ugh," she mutters, wringing her hands and pacing erratically. Then she melts downward toward a full nervous breakdown.

From a puff of orange smoke, Imaginary-Kendra flies up in front of Audra. "Don't be a wimp," she says, unsympathetically. "Sure, you're doomed but, come on, haven't you outgrown that book by now?"

Audra looks under her trembling arm to realize she has been clutching her Circus Elephant book. It has become quite a security blanket over the years. So much so that she often grabs it subconsciously.

She pulls it out and scans its pages in the light of a lightning flash from the window. She smiles at the picture of Elphie and Chimpy, soaked, cheering in the rain.

"Remember," Imaginary-Kendra continues, "that one time after mom and dad read us that story? The three of us ran out into the rain and played all day? We used to like each other. Whatever happened to the three of us?"

Audra hangs her head and slogs off toward her bed. "I wish I knew," she mutters to herself.

Wrapping a blanket around her whole body, Audra lays on her bed and stares out the window at the pouring rain. She can almost hear her and her sisters calling back from her memory, shouting with glee as they danced in the storm of childhood. What did happen to the three of them? What had made Natalia and Kendra bicker so? And why was Audra always stuck in the middle? A real teardrop glides down her cheek, lit by the raindrop-smeared light from the window. Soon her eyelids droop, her thoughts blur, and she falls to sleep, her wet clothes dampening the bed-linens.

"Ooo hah hoo!"

"Aah hoo!"

"Ooo aah!

Audra's eyes burst open. She sits straight up in her bed. While her eyes adjust to the sunlight shining into her room, she squints and looks around to discover a troop of monkeys swinging from the hanging lamp.

Several of the monkeys grab the last few boxes and cans out of the empty, open cupboards and escape out through the open window.

"Wait!" Audra leaps from her bed and chases the remaining monkeys around the room, "That's MY food." She grabs the first book she can get her hands on and swings it at the monkeys. But before she can catch any of them, they all escape.

Audra stands alone in the middle of the messy

room, panting and staring in disbelief at her open, empty cupboards. From where did the monkeys come? Did they have some connection to that mysterious man last night? Did he have some link to the vines covering her home?

She looks down at the book in her hand and notices it is an old copy of *Robinson Crusoe* (about a man who survived for years on a deserted island). Imaginary-Kendra suddenly pops out of the spine of the book.

"Great idea," Imaginary-Kendra shouts, "It's time for a full investigation! Find their monkey nest and squash it."

"So violent!" Imaginary-Natalia pops out next to Kendra and says, "Look, Audra, if the island savages find you they'll kill you. Find them, wait until they are asleep, and then you can chicken out like you always do." Imaginary-Kendra roars with laughter while Imaginary-Natalia waits for the punchline to set in Audra's mind. "Come on. I'm joking. Go get your stuff back, you ninny."

Audra nods, in route to the bathroom, and sets the book and her sisters on the bed. She wraps her hair into a bun as she hurries, shuts the door for a few moments, and following the sounds of running water, she exits, delicately weaving a flower into her hair bun. Little lovely touches like that always helped her feel at least a bit better.

In her march toward the door, she picks up her copy of *The Circus Elephant*, clutching it like a little girl carries her security blanket.

She unbolts the door. She walks out toward the forest. It is time to solve the mysteries of the previous night. And hopefully, she'll do it without anyone seeing her.

Chapter 7: Unlocking The Island's Secrets

Deep in the tropical forest, Audra sneaks about, continuing her investigation. The sun, shining through the leaves, scatters small splashes of light all around her. She carefully tiptoes around the fallen branches and between the trees. She whips around nervously at any sound or movement: a frog, a falling leaf, a couple of birds. Still, every time she scans the scenery, she appears to be completely alone.

Her stomach rumbles as she stumbles upon a big, beautiful coconut. With her tongue between her lips, she tries to open the coconut with her fingers — no success. She smashes it against a rock with all her might, causing it to crack. Water gushes out. In her attempt to get a drink, she gets most of the water on her clothes and only a drop into her dry mouth.

A distant sound startles her. She tosses the coconut into the air. It lands on some rocks several feet away, and the coconut splits in half to reveal its tender white fruit. But Audra, busy scanning her surroundings, doesn't notice the food. She quickly continues deeper into her forest search.

Again and again, she scans the wild scenery, apparently alone.

But in the shadows of the boulders and larger trees, several shadowy, strangely-dressed figures sneak about, spying on Audra. When she looks away, they rush forward to keep up with her. When she looks back, they duck behind the nearest large object.

Finally, Audra sees one of the figures dart out from its hiding place. She didn't know whether it was the same man from last night. If she looks long enough, she might not get away. Audra dashes away, deeper into the forest. Ten figures spring out from their hiding places and pursue her.

Who are these people?

Over a log, around a large boulder, up a small hill, Audra runs with all her might. She comes to a river and spots a vine conveniently tied to a branch beside her. Audra unties it. Just as her pursuers catch up to her, she swings across to the other side of the river. With only a glance at the group of people stalled at the river back behind her, Audra continues her escape. After running thirty feet more, she halts in front of a towering wall of rock with a cave at the base.

Human-made mirrors line the rock walls of the entrance to the cave. After Audra runs straight inside, she finds herself surrounded with reflections of herself. The light from a few torches scatters throughout the reflections of the many cave mirrors, creating the illusion of thousands of torches. Their reflections repeat forever into the distance. What a strange turn of events. Where did these torches come from?

Every few steps, as she frantically searches for a way through the maze, she runs into one of her reflections, or she nearly burns herself on a torch. Backward, forward, sideways. No matter how she walks, she constantly bumps into the walls. She runs into one mirror so hard that she flops to the ground, feet over her head, and tips one of the torches over. She rolls over in the dirt and catches the torch before it hits the ground. As she balances it back into its hole, her face lights up with an idea. As long as she looks away from the mirrors, she may be able to find her way out.

She crawls, focusing on the ground. She clambers forward on her hands and knees with the torch poles as her guide. After bumping into only one more mirror, she finally emerges into a new stretch of daylit forest.

Rumbles of approaching, running feet echo through the cave behind her.

"Ahoy!" shouts a strangely dressed man, who pops out in front of her, juggling five large, colorful balls. Audra, startled, backs up against a wall built of faded, multicolored boards. This slouchy, turtle-like man circles her, with a giant grin etched into his face and smile wrinkles carved deep into his squinting eyes. He tosses one ball to Audra. She throws it back as quickly as possible. While she is switching her Circus Elephant book to her other underarm, he tosses another one of his juggling balls. She fumbles it and accidentally throws her book back instead. She reaches to get it back just as the juggler's eyes open wide at the sound of twenty echoing footsteps.

Ten other enthusiastic people pop out of the cave behind her. The turtle juggler runs away. Audra chases the turtle man. The others chase after Audra, shouting random phrases.

"Welcome!"

"Don't be afraid!"

"Hey, Lady!"

"Look what we can do!"

"Wait for us, Lady!"

"You like clowns?!"

The juggler remarkably continues juggling while running down a circle of human-made

ramps, which connect to the cliffs and spiral down through the forest.

"My book! Please!" Audra shouts forward. "I need it!"

The juggler suddenly stops at the edge of a big dropoff.

Audra charges toward him at full speed and successfully seizes her book, but her momentum is too fast to stop. The juggler and the other circus folk reach after her as she falls into the misty air.

Stiff and wide-eyed, she plummets 50 feet down toward the forest floor. At least, it looks like the forest floor until she sinks into the dirty fabric of a trampoline, which then launches her upward. She soars toward the sky. Several flashes of trapeze artists draped in wild fabrics whiz past her face shouting "welcome" in various languages:

"Buenas Dias!"

"Bien Venue!"

"Willkommen!

A female trapeze artist, hanging by her legs, catches one of Audra's arms with both hands. Together they swing across a village of treehouses made from a mishmash of circus wagons, set pieces, and ocean ship segments. Audra marvels at the bursts of color, the walkways connecting the treehouses, and the vibrant characters scattered all over the village. Most of these people look back at her and wave with wild enthusiasm. Dizzy from all the swinging, Audra wishes this will end.

There is too much attention, too much color, too much craziness. Audra thinks this must be a dream. But when she closes and opens her eyes, trying to wake up, the madness only continues.

The trapeze artist gently places Audra on a platform high above the people. Audra finally releases the breath she has been holding. She takes one look at the tightrope stretching from her platform to another platform fifteen feet away and turns immediately. The bulkiest, most towering brick of a woman she's ever seen stands there with her welcoming arms outstretched, "Seja Bem Vinda, fofa!" Audra nearly bends entirely backward and meets eyes with this magnificent Brazilian giant dressed in zebra stripes.

Balance lost, Audra stumbles backward and finds herself five feet onto the tightrope. Terror fills her soul. The onlookers gasp as Audra struggles to

keep her balance, to gain her footing, to walk back to that platform and escape the dangerous tightrope.

"A i y a i y a i y a i - yai!" they scream as she swings her arms backward while tipping forward.

"Ohh!" they shout as she successfully takes a step forward.

"Yay!" they cheer as a male trapeze artist whisks her away from danger and toward a safe, stable platform below.

With her feet on solid ground, Audra smiles as she catches her breath. Her whole body trembles, but she knows if she is going to escape, she must act now. She ducks into a small alleyway where no one is watching her, where she can take some time to recover and think of some way to get out of here.

"Hello," says a calm, soothing, male voice beside her. She flinches away, not sure if she can trust even the mildest voice in this circumstance.

"Don't fear. I want to help you," says the man, as he steps out into her view.

Something looks familiar about his appearance: goggles, hat, a beard, and bee motifs in his outfit.

"And you can help me," the man continues.

Audra, though still recovering from confusion, feels an emotional weight of distrust and takes a step backward. She finds herself up against a wall, cornered. She looks to the side for some way to escape.

"Come with me," the man says reaching out his hand, "I need you to show me how to use that machine of yours. Then we can come to an arrangement."

"What?" Audra whispers, staring up at the man. The brilliant sun reflects from the metal scraps above them, silhouetting him perfectly. Her mind flashes back to the shadowy figure whose silhouette she saw stealing her device in the lightning storm.

"YOU!" she shouts in disgust. Audra unleashes her fury, swinging her circus book blindly in his direction. "You stole—"

"Borrowed," the man clarifies.

"And my house!" Audra shouts, still swinging blindly.

"We decorated it ... to hide it from the crooked fishermen."

Audra stops. "Fishermen?"

"Yes," says the man, snatching the book from her hands. "If you calm down we'll get this all explained and settled."

Audra tilts her head and stares at him for just a moment, trying to figure out whether he is trustworthy. He looks down at the book, curious. Nervously, she replies, "Maybe ... if you give my book back."

"Interesting! You interested in the circus?" The Ringmaster asks, flipping through the pages.

"No," Audra replies, trying to snatch the book back. But the Ringmaster holds it high above his head where she can't reach.

A door opens just behind and to the left of the man. The turtle juggler pops his head out. "Ringmaster!"

"Yes?" The Ringmaster turns to answer him.

Audra seizes the moment, ducks, and runs past both of them. She'll have to get the book back later, but at least she escaped the villain. She runs around the right turn, then the left, and falls right through a trap door, landing her right in the middle of what looks like an old-fashioned funhouse.

Audra stares forward at an overwhelming sight: six hallways filled with flashing colors, rotating patterns, twists and turns in every direction.

"This way," shouts a young woman from the hallway to the left. Audra hesitates for a moment, looking the girl up and down. Her costume was inspired by a jellyfish, with hanging strips of fabric and even decorative fish in the stingers. Well, she looks trustworthy enough. Audra turns and runs beside this Jellyfish Girl down a hallway.

"Dive into the water just around there," the Jellyfish Girl instructs as they run around the corner. The girl dives right into a pool of water.

Audra stops right at the pool's edge.

She paces around it nervously, debating whether or not she should follow. Far behind her, an opening door squeaks and circus people come running into the fun house. That is all the motivation she needs. Audra shuts her eyes and collapses to the ground.

The Jellyfish Girl returns, her head popping up from the water. "Come on!"

Audra nods and slips into the water. She swims beside her guide through the underwater tunnel bathed in refreshing sea-green light. The Jellyfish Girl glides and spins through the water, the most graceful swimmer imaginable. Audra, on the other hand, does a slow doggy paddle.

They emerge from the pool on the other side where the human-made walls end and the forest continues. As they wring out their clothes, a similarly-dressed Jellyfish twin runs up to them, gushing with joy, "Oh, you brought her!" She circles Audra, studying every detail. "You are the perfect canvas," she says to Audra at a frantic, energetic pace. "Your slender physique ... this long auburn hair ... I know the perfect animal to inspire your costume. Let's show her, Shelly!"

Her wet sister hops up straight, "Okay, Nelly!"

Audra rolls her eyes. Every time she meets somebody she feels she can trust, they end up wanting to use her for something. She backs up against the wall, inching to the side.

In a mad rush, Nelly tosses some clothes and trimmings turning Shelly into something resembling a jellyfish with an elephant nose. They then turn to Audra, saying in unison, "How's this?"

Audra is gone.

"Be sure to watch out for the tiger!" Shelly shouts after her.

Upon hearing the warning, Audra looks behind herself and runs right off a leafy ledge and into a tangled mess of vines. She grasps them and pulls them away, struggling and wiggling until she breaks free. Fleeing through the forest, even now that no one pursues her, she continually checks behind her, paranoid and pumped with adrenaline.

Her body jerks, her lungs heave, but she keeps running until tears leak out from her eyes.

Her lungs rasp as her pace slows to a jog.

What an exhausting and crazy day she has had, an exhausting couple of days. Traveling and getting used to a new home can be tiring enough, but add strange sightings, a complete home makeover, an intruder, monkeys, and the insanity of the circus - that has the makings of a nightmare. Hopefully, it's over.

Into a clearing of trees, Audra slogs along, feeling quite dizzy and watching her feet. And when she looks up, she beholds a giant, plump, peacock-ish creature.

Nope, it's not over.

Here stands another over-enthusiastic circus person. Maybe Audra can sneak past her.

Audra tiptoes around, toward the trees to the left, trying to tame her heavy breathing and never taking her eyes off the creature, person, whatever it was.

Suddenly it turns and looks at Audra, revealing a delightfully plump female face. Both Audra and the Peacock Girl scream and turn away. The Peacock Girl staggers in one direction and hides behind a tree. Audra does the same, stumbling and panting through the whole escape.

Audra leans against her hiding tree with her arms rigidly pressed to her side. Her eyelids alternate between closing and fluttering open as she shakes her head in random directions. She melts down the tree trunk into a crumpled mess at the bottom.

Two minutes pass before Audra's breathing slows to an average pace. Her eyes start to dart, her brow creases, and her mind reviews what just occurred. Curiosity pulls her attention back behind her hiding tree.

From the tree across the clearing, the Peacock Girl peeks in Audra's direction. With only a slight delay, Audra peaks around her tree. The moment they see each other, they slip back into their hiding spots.

Again, they both slowly peek around, and in perfect synchronization, they hide once more.

Even though Audra is quite lean and the Peacock Girl is delightfully plump, somehow it's as if they are looking in a mirror: both of them slide their backs up their tree. Both clutch their clothes and tighten their shoulders. Both slowly creep around their trees to take a peak. Both faces light up with intrigue and rather than hiding again, they both step outward. Moving at a similar pace and in the same posture and even blinking within the same millisecond, they continue to approach, tilting their heads in various directions. They circle round, coming within just a few feet.

Then they pause.

They stare.

"Somehow," the Peacock Girl whispers in a timid voice, "you remind me of my mother."

Audra's face fills with wonder. "Strange," she says in a breathy voice, "I was going to say the same thing … but that's quite unusual since you could easily be my daughter."

"Really?" the Peacock Girl steps back. "But you look so young."

"You must be somewhere around twenty, and I'm more than double that age."

"Hmm," says the Peacock Girl.

"Hmm," Audra imitates.

Both of them stand there, waiting for the other to speak. Usually, Audra feels so unsure and uncomfortable around people, but there is something so unassuming about this girl.

"You know," Audra starts to tell her, "I never have—"

Distant shouts instantly destroy the peaceful vibe in the forest clearing. "I see her! She's over there!"

Thirty smiling people bound down through the trees. Audra panics and immediately runs away. The Peacock Girl starts after her, but then she stops and turns back toward the group.

"Please," she begs, her voice lost in the passing crowd. "Let's leave her alone for a while." These circus comrades run past her without any acknowledgment. She sighs and jogs forward after them.

Out of the trees, Audra runs across the beach toward her home. Exhaustion overtakes her. She grasps at the railing of her ramp. But a simple glance back to her gleeful pursuers gives her the last boost of adrenaline she needs. She staggers up the ramp, runs into the open door, and deadbolt locks herself inside.

The moment of silence ends with eager circus faces popping up in her windows.

"Don't be afraid," someone shouts.

"Let's be friends," another yells.

Audra doesn't want friends. She wants peace. She wants to be left alone.

Audra limps toward every last window and shuts the curtains on every single one of those anxious, joy-filled faces.

BOOOOOOOM! A colossal explosion sounds in the distance, followed by the panicked shouting from the circus people outside. Audra opens the curtains to see them scattering, running off in various directions. With her cheek pressed to the glass, she watches the people clamor away into the forest.

"We should go too," says a deep male voice behind Audra. She leaps up three feet in the air, catching only a glimpse of the massive silhouetted thief who has again been waiting in the shadows of her home. She screams, scrambles to flee, and bumps her head on a hanging lamp. Knocked unconscious, she teeters and topples toward the hardwood floor.

The large man rushes forward and catches her. He picks her up and carries her as if he were moving a delicate child, toward the door.

"Poor thing," he says to unconscious Audra as

he unbolts the door. "They're just desperate for attention..."

He carries her down, turns toward the forest, and disappears into the trees.

Chapter 8: The Ringmaster

The scene is white, like an empty page. Elphie the circus elephant sneaks into view. Chimpy comes tiptoeing in from the whiteness on the other side. He takes Elphie by the hand and leads her to a black charcoal drawing of a door. They open the door and peek inside to see an empty theater scene, also hand-drawn in black on white. Chimpy runs around the circus ring doing tricks for Elphie's entertainment. Her face lights up. She claps her hands.

Chimpy runs and grabs a big ball from the middle of the circus ring and jumps on top. He rolls it over and Elphie leaps right up there with him. They begin their routine.

As they practice their first trick together — where Elphie balances upside-down with her hand on the ball and Chimpy balances on her feet — fourteen monkeys swing in out of nowhere. They interlink with Chimpy into a circular formation, balancing atop Elphie's feet.

Elphie tips out of balance and her arm trembles to hold the weight while staying centered on the ball. They sway to the left, to the right, front and back. Elphie's hand slips. Her screaming mouth smacks down on the ball. Her lips stretch and suck the over-sized ball into her stomach, making her round and bouncy. The weight of the monkeys falls upon her, and squash, SPRING, they launch upward.

The monkeys ride the Elphie Ball as they break through the white theater roof and BOUNCE out into the empty whiteness. The monkeys relish the thrill, but Elphie does not. They plummet downward, BOUNCE up again, hang in the air, plummet, bounce back, hang, plummet, and BOUNCE again.

A giant pair of hands catches Elphie and the monkeys as if they were a baseball. A giant, red-smoke, Kendra face glares down.

"Wake up, sleepy head!"

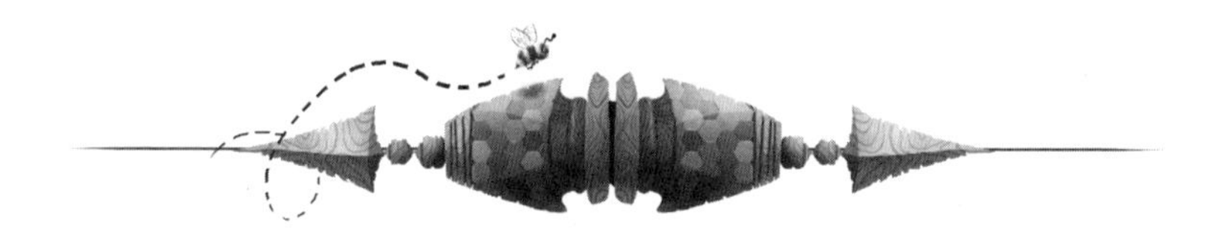

From a dingy, large bed, Audra sits straight up, sweat droplets trailing from her brow. A headache immediately fills her head. Everything in the surrounding room appears dark and blurry.

"Ugh," she moans. Holding her throbbing forehead, she flops back down to the pillow.

"She's awake," shouts an eager young voice. A blurry, boyish figure hops out of the fuzzy chair beside the bed and skips over to a much larger figure standing near the fireplace. Audra squints, and the more significant figure gradually shifts into focus, revealing the silhouette of that same man who has distressed her three times in the past twenty-four hours.

"Oh no!" Audra throws off her covers and scrambles to escape from her bed. But as she stands her legs tremble and she falls off balance. The large man bounds over to catch her and gently helps her sit back on the bed.

"Not so fast," he says in his surprisingly gentle voice.

Audra slaps his wrists and shrinks away. "Hands off, thief." She tries to stand and escape again, but the dizziness pulls her back down.

"He's no thief," says the eager young man, dressed to resemble a tiger. "He's our Ringmaster. He's master of this whole island."

Audra scowls, folding her arms in complete disagreement. No, she was the person who bought this island. And no creeper, no thief was going to be the master of her island. She scans the cluttered, dingy room. Animal pelts, hooks, and gadgets litter the walls, but there is no sign of her high-tech communication device.

"So where is it, master thief?"

"I was planning to return your machine," the Ringmaster says, irritated, then continues in a calmer voice, "But first I need to know if I can trust you."

Audra cocks her head, perplexed. What kind of fool did this man think she was?

A bunch of monkeys swing into the room and leap toward a considerable stack of food in the corner. "Shoo!" shouts the Ringmaster, bounding toward them. "You'll get some when I give you some!"

The monkeys shriek and scramble to various corners of the room.

"My food!" Audra shouts, her shock increasing. "Did you train the monkeys to steal that too?"

"Look," says the Ringmaster, a little tenser, "I've worked for years to build a life here for my people, to protect them from the outside world and I just need to make sure your presence will benefit my people and not ruin them."

"This guy is a real crook," says Imaginary-Kenda,

peaking out in a puff of smoke from inside Audra's imagination. "Maybe he thinks you're going to phone America and give some reporter the juicy details on his front page secret."

"Or maybe he's a pirate!" Imaginary-Natalia peaks out as well. "Maybe he wants you to join them and keep their secrets. But the moment you budge, he'll cuff you and make you his slavc."

"Absolutely not!" Audra shouts, surprising both the Ringmaster and the Tiger Boy. She continues in her usual timid tone, "I don't know what kind of crooked, villainous scheme you are trying to pull here, but...I..." Her words fade into frustrated breaths.

She wants to stand up to him. She wants to command him to give her device back and let her go free, but her timidity starts to set back in, and she can see the Ringmaster's face has flushed red with anger.

"Look, woman," the Ringmaster shouts. "No one calls me crooked or a thief, not after all I've sacrificed for this people!"

Audra's imaginary sisters both giggle.

The Ringmaster continues, speaking through

tight teeth and a fake grin. "Look. Things are starting to look grim around here, and I can't seem to figure out how your machine works. Now if I could get you to call out on your machine and order some more food, I could save my people from starvation."

"STARVATION?!" The Tiger Boy nearly jumps up from his chair.

"Hush, boy," the Ringmaster scolds, "We're not starving yet."

"What I meant is," Audra says, nervous and timid as ever.

"What?" snaps the Ringmaster.

"Don't blow this, Audra," says Imaginary-Kendra, popping out of the Ringmaster's beard.

Imaginary-Natalia skates around the brim of his hat, "Poor Audra, never knows what to say." Both sisters laugh.

"Well?" the Ringmaster asks impatiently.

"Well," Audra says timidly, "I'm not sure I trust..." She pauses as the Ringmaster's face scrunches in anger and she sees her imaginary sisters freeze, eyes full of anticipation. Audra groans inside. She never does well under this kind of pressure.

"I mean I … I just want to be alone. I wouldn't be ... a fan of ... joining the circus."

"What's wrong with the circus?!" The Ringmaster jumps up, red in the face. "You know what? I am just too mad to handle this right now." He paces the room, talking to himself. "I'll calm down, and then I'll come back. Then I'll show you I'm not so bad."

Audra's imaginary sisters parachute off of the Ringmaster shouting, "BOMBED IT!"

The Ringmaster opens the door and pauses. "You keep an eye on her, Andrew," he says as exits and slams the door behind him, reducing the shoulder sisters to dust.

Andrew, the Tiger Boy, turns to Audra, who buries her face in her hands. He puts his hand on her shoulder. She looks up at his face, at his gesture of comfort.

He seems like a sweet boy. Maybe he will be willing to help.

"Will you help me up?" she asks, still rubbing her face. Andrew hesitantly complies, holding her by the shoulders. "Is there a back door?" she asks as she stands.

"Yes, but..." Andrew says as he helps her walk toward the back wall. "You won't let us starve, will you? Ringmaster just isn't used to no disrespect. We only decorated your house to throw off the enemy. And we were only borrowing your machine." He pulls back a buffalo hide to reveal the back door.

"I'm sorry, of course, I wouldn't let anyone starve to death, but how can I trust what he, what you, what anyone says?" Audra says wearily, "I just need time to think about what to do about all of this."

As Andrew reaches for the doorknob, the

Peacock Girl's face peeks in through the round window. Upon seeing Audra, she immediately opens the door.

"Penny?" Andrew says, surprised.

"Peacock?" Audra exclaims at the same time.

"Yes," the girl smiles. "Penny. Peacock. I thought you might like a few of your books." Penny hands Audra her Circus Elephant along with the green book about Princess Genevieve.

"Lovely! Can you also help me escape?" Audra asks.

"Escape?" Penny gives Audra a puzzled expression, "I guess so."

Audra takes a few wobbly steps forward then turns back. "Thank you, Andrew," she says as she pats the Tiger Boy on the cheek. "I'll make sure you don't starve. If that's the true problem."

"It is," Andrew responds.

Penny offers Audra an arm, but Audra moves forward on her own, quickly gaining confidence in her footing. Penny leads her down a series of suspended walkways through the trees on the edge of the circus community.

Multiple branches and their large leaves give

them plenty of camouflage from the circus village's view. Audra's concerned scowl gradually softens on her journey through the softly-lit forest. As the spring returns to her step, she smiles a pleasant smile. At the end of their refreshing stroll, they walk through the back door of the smallest tree-house in the whole community and step inside.

Hundreds of wall-pinned drawings catch Audra's immediate attention. She walks over to them, her eyes scanning them in wonder, her mouth in a foolish grin.

Penny lunges toward the open can of beans on her bedside table. Sitting squarely on her bouncy bed, she scoops heaping spoonfuls of those beans into her mouth as if she hasn't eaten for days.

Audra continues to study the drawings in awe: several detailed plans for seafaring ships, calculations for individual pieces of those ships, with lists of the necessary materials. "Did you draw these?" she asks, without wavering in her attention to the renderings.

"Ohh Wesh," Penny says with her mouth full of beans, "Ahhhi fwooo mooophu Juumm. Meehh wwooeeem—"

Penny stops and swallows as Audra turns toward her with a puzzled expression. "Oh, I'm sorry. Did you need some?"

Audra, hungrier than even she realizes, leaps over to grab the can. Without a word, she reaches inside, pulls out the last two remaining beans, and throws them toward the back of her throat. For a moment she savors those beans, eyes closed, tongue licking her lips. She then looks back into the empty can and slouches in great disappointment.

"Sorry," says Penny. "We only get a few rations a day."

Audra slumps down on the bed beside Penny, who simultaneously stands. Penny walks toward the drawings with slow steps and sad eyes.

"So who drew those?" Audra asks carefully.

"I've dreamt of engineering ships since I was a little girl." Pointing to a group of drawings, Penny recounts, "My William helped me draw the first few drawings, and I keep drawing more. I can't help myself. "

"Who is William?" Audra whispers intrigued.

"My husband." Tears fill Penny's eyes, and she clenches her stomach with both hands. "He wanted to see the world, I wanted to stay here, felt I needed to stay here." She continues with great bitterness in her voice, "He went to go talk to the Ringmaster and then I..." The tears now roll down her cheeks and seep into her lips. She cries so hard that she can barely finish her sentence, "... never... saw him again..."

Audra sits, just staring at Penny, opening her mouth occasionally with no words to say. Frozen and blushing, she watches as Penny helplessly collapses against the wall, sobbing deeply. A sudden rage fills her whole body.

"So what did the Ringmaster do?" Audra asks.

Penny attempts to speak, but the message comes out as a tearful squeak.

"I bet the Ringmaster banished him," Audra stands up, outraged.

"What?" Penny looks up, surprised.

"He's such a secretive, scheming man. Maybe he was worried that William would expose the island secrets. Maybe he ... you know." Audra turns, and with an absolute look of terror in her eyes, draws a line across her throat.

"No, no, the Ringmaster isn't like that." Penny continues speaking, only a little weepy. "Someone told me they saw him leave on a boat."

"Probably with a vow of secrecy. A vow to never return."

"No, no, I'm sorry," Penny says, walking toward Audra and rubbing away the tears. "It's only been six months, but I haven't had anyone I felt I could talk to."

"I'm glad you did," Audra says, pacing the room.

"I feel like it was my fault. Maybe I should have found a better way to break the news about our..."

Audra, who has been thinking, not listening, nearly leaps when an idea hits her. "I've got it!"

Penny, slightly stunned, finishes her sentence, "...baby."

"You know this island well, right?" Audra blurts, not even realizing Penny has revealed some ultra-personal information. “I need to find a place where no one will follow me, where I can find some food and have a few days to think alone.”

Penny looks at Audra with an injured expression. “Did you just hear me? I—”

Audra quickly adds, “But you can come.”

Penny looks away to the corner of the room. Audra realizes she just did something wrong, but what?

“I mean…” Audra continues, puzzled. “I’m no good at things like this, Penny, but maybe…”

Without a word, Penny stands up and walks to the corner of her room. Audra sighs and looks back at the drawings.

“I interrupted you, didn’t I?” Audra says, deeply disappointed in herself.

Without a word, Penny picks up a spear and a knapsack. She tosses the bag to Audra and walks out. Audra sighs and follows.

“Maybe you can tell me what you were about to say,” Audra says hopefully, touching Penny’s arm.

“Maybe later,” Penny responds. “I’m not used to opening up like this.” She pulls away and walks out her front door.

Silent, Audra follows Penny. Every few minutes, Audra fidgets with her lips, thinking of something to say. But nothing seems right. Eventually, Audra embraces the silence.

The sun is high, the air pleasant. In the late afternoon, Penny stops to climb a tree and drop some coconuts to the ground. Audra puts the fruit in their sack, and with only a smile and a nod, they carry on.

As storm clouds gather and the sky becomes overcast, Penny catches the only fish in a pond with her spear. Audra passes that time tossing disapproving looks at the storm clouds. It just rained one or two days ago. She grumbles, "Does it have to rain again?"

Penny tosses the wriggling fish in the bag and presses onward. Audra continues to follow, still with no conversation. When the dark, heavy clouds turn golden, Penny and Audra arrive at the entrance of a large cave. Penny gestures for Audra to enter, sets her sack down just inside, and turns to walk away.

Audra fidgets around nervously as she watches Penny leave. "Wait!" she says.

"I'm okay," Penny says, turning around quickly and speaking with great tension in her voice. "I'm just concerned about you staying here all alone."

"Right, so maybe..." Audra considers inviting Penny to stay, but throughout the day she hasn't been able to think of anything but her blunder with Penny. Maybe they both need some alone time to recharge.

"Just make sure you build a fire in case the tiger comes around," Penny says.

"Tiger?" Audra suddenly feels nervous.

"You'll be alright," Penny says, backing away. "We'll chat soon."

"Tomorrow?" Audra blurts out, nervous at the thought of a tiger.

Penny turns away quickly and hurries off as it starts to rain. Audra follows her a few steps. She calls out, "Are you sure you don't want to stay?" But pouring rain drowns out her voice and instantly drenches every inch of her clothes. With Penny out of her sight, Audra turns and slogs toward the cave.

It's not exactly the best place to stay dry. Because of the many openings in the cave ceiling, the rain falls into several pools on the rocky floor.

"A fire..." Audra mutters to herself as she carries her bag of food to a dry spot and sits with her legs crossed. She opens the bag, pulling out a couple coconuts and a tiny, slimy salmon. Her gag reflex kicks in. She covers her nose and mouth to stop herself from vomiting.

She returns the fish and wraps that bag as tightly as she can. She picks up the coconuts and moves to a dry spot, far away from the fish. There she breaks several coconuts on the stone floor, struggles to catch any leaking coconut milk, and eats as much of the firm fruit as she can scrape off the shells.

Seeing the rain has stopped, she crawls over to one of the small cavern pools and scoops some water into her mouth, finally quenching her ardent thirst. She looks out the cave's entrance and thinks of Penny, wondering if she was drenched from the storm, shivering from the cold. Audra wishes she had asked Penny to stay. Maybe they could have talked more about her tragic romance. Maybe Audra could have helped Penny. Well, that will be the first item of business next time they meet.

Audra would love to have her help right now. Sadly, she has no idea how to build a fire, especially with wet wood.

Audra scans the cave, looking for a log or a branch or even a scrap she could burn. But with only a bit of sunlight and the rain pouring on, she gives up. At least, with the last bit of sunlight, she could read and hopefully find some inspiration.

Audra pulls out her green book about Princess Genevieve and skips to the part in the cave, hoping it might give her some ideas about how to solve her current predicament. As she reads, she imagines herself as the main character, as always:

Beneath her father's castle, deep in the dampness of the endless caverns, Genevieve-Audra tip-toes through the darkness with only a candle to light her footsteps. Drops of water fall on her nose, on her hair, on her dress. Dripping sounds reverberate from the rocks and cavern puddles. She

holds her left hand above the flame to protect the flame from the fate of extinguishment.

As she comes near a shadowy corner, she hears the sound of someone breathing.

"Prince Ruben?" Genevieve-Audra calls out.

No voice returns her call — only breathing.

Genevieve-Audra's whole body fills with terror, "Please be Prince Ruben," she gasps.

"Genevieve!" Prince Ruben's voice shouts from the opposite direction. She turns to see him running furiously with a bright torch lighting his way. "Run!"

Genevieve-Audra succumbs to the immediate temptation to look back to the shadowy corner. The breathing turns to an ominous growl. Steam emerges from a dragon's nostrils. Its wings expand outward as its head moves up toward the cavern ceiling. Genevieve-Audra staggers backward, tense with fear.

"Run!"

"Well that was a bad idea," Audra mutters as she quickly shuts the book and looks toward every shadow in the surrounding cave. Her whole body trembles at the thought of what could be lurking there. A cool breeze covers Audra in a rainy mist. Chills run down her arms. Dread drops down to the dregs of her stomach.

She releases her grip on the book and lets it fall to the ground. Reading wasn't going to help her escape this situation.

"You could use the book to start a fire," Imaginary-Kendra whispers into Audra's ear.

Audra grimaces at the thought. She never imagined it would ever cross her mind.

"You've gotta admit," Imaginary-Natalia peeks out from behind Kendra, "After reading it for the fourth time, your book does pale in comparison to what you've just lived through."

Audra smiles at this new thought. The book has lived a good life. And surviving the night was the only way she'd read it a fifth time.

So at that moment she does something she never thought she'd do. She kneels, opens the book before her, and clacks two rocks together in an attempt to make some sparks. The clack echoes through the cave, but no flashes appear. She tries again.

Clack!

Tiny Sparks. Again!

CLACK!

After insufficient sparks and an over-sufficient echo, a growl comes from the shadows.

Audra's entire body turns to the sound. The chills, dread, and the trembling all return.

From the back of the cave, an orange-and-black-striped-tiger struts in, his eyes focused on the sack of fish.

Audra freezes at the sight of him, her brain calculating a thousand ways any attempt to escape would likely end in failure.

The tiger rips the sack open and devours the fish.

As it licks its lips, its eyes meet Audra's. The tiger immediately bolts toward her. Audra jumps to her feet and lets out a raspy scream. In full panic, she stumbles backward toward the cavern wall, never taking her eyes away from her ferocious cave-mate.

As it happens in momentous occasions, time seems to move much slower as the tiger bounds toward her, claws out, and teeth bared, eyes intense, growling with pleasure.

At that vital moment when the tiger's claw is inches away from tearing Audra's skin, a shadowy figure jumps between them. A stream of fire follows. The tiger stops and scrambles away. Audra observes, stunned, as the Ringmaster howls, swinging a lamp on a chain, drawing rings of fire in the air.

The tiger backs away, batting at the fire with its paws and growling through its sharp smile. The Ringmaster continues to advance. Audra finally releases a burst of breath and sinks to the ground. The stress of the past few days, the hunger and the confusion, has all wholly exhausted her strength. Through dreary eyes, she watches the Ringmaster tame the beast.

The tiger takes ten more backward steps out through the entrance, to the edge of a mild cliff. His foot slips and he slides, clawing and growling, down a fairly steep hill. He lands on his back, scrambles to his feet, and flees into the forest.

The Ringmaster strides back into the cave to extinguish the fire of his lamp in the pool. The water evaporates into a cloud of steam. He walks over to Audra, who lies passed out on the stone floor. As he lifts her in his arms, she babbles deliriously, "I'm okay. I need a bite to eat and then I'll be fine." He nods in acknowledgment, retrieves her possessions, and heads out of the cave. She closes her eyes. Her whole body hangs limp and unconscious for a moment. Then she raises her head and pats his muscular arm. "Thank…you…" Then she collapses into a deep sleep.

The moonlight gently bathes the forest in pale blue. The Ringmaster carries her for hours past the river and the coconut trees.

At last, they return to circus village.

Chapter 9: Join The Circus?

In the middle of a prairie wheat meadow, surrounded by a bright fog, in a patch of gold in the middle of endless whiteness, a green-leaved tree shades an 8-year-old girl from the sun. There she sits on a log, reading a brand-new copy of The Circus Elephant. Another little girl sneaks up behind her and jumps out to scare her.

"Aaaahhh," little Audra screams, "Kendra!"

A third little girl runs by, ripping the book from Audra's hands.

"Give that back, Natalia!" little Audra shouts as she chases her sisters in circles around the meadow. In a swirling second, the meadow transforms into a high school hallway filled with teenagers. Led by Natalia and Kendra, they encircle Audra, jeering at her with mischief in their eyes.

"Show them!" teenage Kendra says through a nasty grin. Teenage Audra cowers, looking around for some way to escape the crowd.

"Yeah," says a boy behind Audra. "We want to see this kiddie book you carry everywhere." As Audra turns toward the boy, Natalia unzips Audra's backpack and yanks out The Circus Elephant.

"Here it is!" Kendra shouts, holding the book in the air. Audra jumps, trying to snag her book. The teenagers laugh.

As Audra catches the book and clutches it to her chest, the teenagers and hallway transform into her father's private study where she sits between her mother and father in the glow of a warm fire.

Tears roll down Audra's cheeks as she confides in her parents. "I don't think I'll ever find my place in this world. No one likes me. They only like to laugh at me."

"Oh Audra," her mother says, embracing her from behind. "There are so many good people in the world who would love you if they got to know you."

"You always say that, and I want to believe it, but I..." Audra says, looking up. Her mother suddenly turns dark and wisps away as the private study transforms into a green-brick funeral home. Audra stands in front of her parent's caskets, her two sisters watching the clock behind her. Audra stands tensely, tears leaking down her cheeks.

The funeral home immediately vanishes in another whirl and becomes a cold, dark room. Audra still clutches The Circus Elephant to her chest. Kendra and Natalia pace the room angrily, followed by men in suits with briefcases.

"AUDRA?" Natalia shrieks out a grown-up-tantrum. "They gave the house to AUDRA?"

"What about the rest of the fortune?" Kendra roars. "Don't I get anything?"

"She's not fit to take care of that house," Natalia continues stomping around the room. "Look at her. It's like she's stuck at age twelve!"

Her sisters, the suits, and the room, all vanish. All goes dark.

Audra rolls over in the dingy, dark bed. The room fills with the voices of young, excited children. Her eyes slowly open and squint as they adjust to the light. She lifts her head to see the familiar scene of the Ringmaster's quarters: The fire in the hearth, the clutter, only two cans left of the stolen food, but the Ringmaster is nowhere to be seen. The children sit in a circle on the floor chatting excitedly about an object they are passing around: a book!

When she sees *The Circus Elephant* embossed on the cover, Audra suddenly sits up in bed and shouts, "Careful!"

Penny walks in from the hallway with a large kettle in her arms. "I keep telling you to leave that alone. That book was given to her by her mother and father." The kids moan as Penny takes the book away and returns it to a wide-eyed Audra.

"How did you...?" Audra whispers.

"I saw the message in the front cover. The picture too." Penny smiles and puts the kettle on the stove.

"Ah good!" sounds the deep, boisterous voice of the Ringmaster as he enters the room. "She's awake." He walks right over to her bedside, "Now that I've saved you twice, you owe your life to this circus." He laughs, but Audra can't tell if he is serious or joking.

Audra makes a pleading look to Penny, who says, "You can't really make her join us."

"Of course I can't," he smiles while motioning to the children, "but they can."

The children follow his cue without hesitation, leaping up from their sitting spots and jumping onto her bed to smother Audra. One hugs her arm. Another hugs her waist. A girl tugs at her hands — a boy tugs at her toes.

Though the kids are adorable, this attention is very distressing to Audra. She has done nothing to deserve it. This must be the Ringmaster's manipulation.

They beg, in rehearsed tones, "Please stay.

Please. Please. Please."

Audra gives them a little smile.

"Maybe I would if truly you had asked it, but I suspect the question comes from someplace else." Audra glares up at the Ringmaster.

"Alright now," The Ringmaster holds onto her arms and leads her out of the bed, "I have more people I'd like you to meet."

"Oh no," Audra mumbles, "I need more rest." She shakes her head and tries to lay back on the bed, but his grip is too strong.

The Ringmaster dismisses her comment. "Too much rest is bad for you."

Audra gives him an unforgiving stare while he drags her out through the front door and into the center of the bustling village. Her legs go weak at the sight of many crowds scattered before the platform where the Ringmaster clears his throat, ready to make his announcement. If he weren't holding her up, she would be melting to the floor. All of the wild headdresses and painted faces turn, looking straight at them. Audra closes her eyes and tries to calm her heavy breathing.

"Ladies and Gentleman! Boys and Girls!" The Ringmaster announces in a booming voice, "I want you to meet the newest member of our loving community…" He stops and looks around, then turns to her and whispers, "What was your name?"

"Aud-," she can barely choke out the second syllable, "-ra."

"Her name is ODD!" He announces, then quickly returns to a whisper, "Really? That's an odd name."

Audra shakes her head and whispers, "Audra." But the Ringmaster doesn't hear.

"Make way!" shouts an old female voice from the back of the main crowd, which parts and separates to watch an old woman on a unicycle riding through, a giraffe-patterned cloak dragging behind her. She flashes her radiant, wide grin around the crowd. "Give me some room, sugar-cubes. You don't want this old lady to break a hip, do ya?"

Audra opens one eye to peek. The other eye quickly follows. Both eyes grow wide at the sight of this old female unicyclist.

The old woman stops right in front of the stage and when her gaze meets Audra's, her otherwise droopy eyelids grow just as wide! And her smile, which doesn't seem like it could get any bigger, spreads wider. "Well!" she exclaims. "She IS odd."

Audra furrows her brow.

The Ringmaster steps between them, "Good morning, Wise One. About Odd's role, I've noticed the animals need some more caretakers. We also need another cook."

The Wise Woman's eyes get droopy and annoyed, but she continues to smile. "I noticed that too, Ringmaster. Now step aside so I can get another look at this lovely apple dumpling."

The Ringmaster rolls his eyes, sighs, and steps aside.

The Wise Woman tosses a crystal ball at Audra, who catches it with her right hand while holding *The Circus Elephant* in the other.

"Nice catch," The Wise Woman comments,

excited as a child on their birthday. "Look in that mystic ball and tell me what you see."

Audra looks around, nervous. The Wise Woman reassures her. "Forget about everyone else. Come closer and tell me what you see in this ball."

Audra moves closer. The whole crowd listens in silence.

The Ringmaster sighs and rolls his eyes again, mumbling, "We go over this every time. There's nothing in there."

"I see," Audra says softly, "reflections and refractions of the world and people around us. That's what crystal does after all. It's lovely that way."

The Ringmaster stares down, slightly stunned.

The Wise Woman's smile disappears. She peers at Audra so intensely, as if trying to see her soul. "I thought so," the woman says. She turns back to the crowd.

"In observation of Odd's scrawny figure, obsession with books, and unique perspective, I would like to announce that I have finally found my replacement. Meet Odd, your new Wise Woman!"

"What?" Audra and the Ringmaster shriek together.

The Wise Woman hops off her unicycle and puts her arms around Audra, leading her. "That's exactly the reaction I'd expect. A truly wise woman doesn't ever think she is wise, I should know! I feel a little dumber every day."

They walk into a unique gazebo where the crowd is lining up to speak to Audra. Clutching her blouse tightly, she scans the line of people. The people gawk at her, pointing and whispering. She makes eye contact with one of them, then quickly looks away.

The Wise Woman sits on a stack of Persian fabric pillows under the gazebo. As she does so, she motions for Audra to take her seat on the larger pillow pile. Audra sits nervously, eyeing the crowd.

"Alright, Odd..." The Wise Woman gleefully says.

"Audra," comes a whispered correction.

"Oh, sorry, Audrey. Let's get you to work!"

Audra asks, horrified, "Right now? Can't I prepare?"

"I'm sure they're just eager to meet you. Our people rarely need any deep advice." The Wise Woman addresses the crowd. "I know many of you are in line to see me, but today we're going to try out our new Wise Woman. Please be gentle. Yes?"

The first man in line steps forward. Audra recognizes him as the turtle-like juggler from the cave of mirrors.

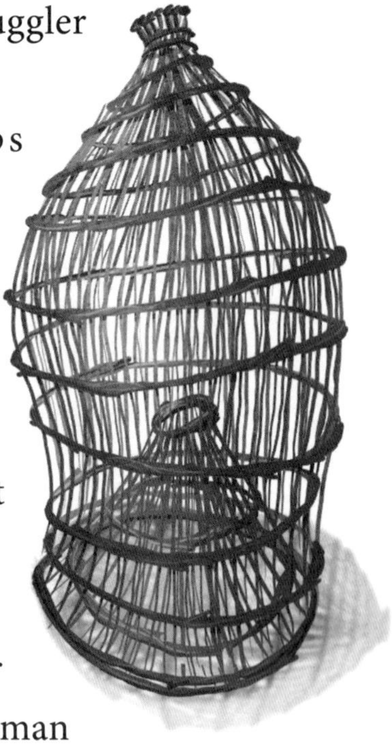

The Turtle Man steps forward again, holding up an empty fish trap. "Our fish supply is almost completely gone. The reef is almost destroyed. I've already come to the Wise Old One about this..." Audra starts to have a panic attack and looks to the Wise Woman, who shuts her eyes and shakes her head. The man continues, "and she told us to be patient while she deliberates, but I fear we might starve if we wait too long. Please help us, fresh, young, Wise One."

Audra looks upward, searching her mind for something useful to stay.

"Also, we don't have enough outhouses," the turtle man continues, gesturing to another long line leading up to an outhouse about fifteen feet away. "We're eating too many coconuts and too little fish and you know what that does..."

They watch as a man opens the door of that distant outhouse and takes one step out, but he suddenly grabs his aching stomach and jumps right back into the outhouse and the door slams behind him. The people in that distant line let out a long groan.

Audra, overwhelmed, collapses back onto the pile of pillows and groans in breathy exasperation, "Why?"

The turtle man looks around in concern.

"Looks like you've already broken our new Wise Woman, Ronald," the Wise Woman tells the turtle man, dryly.

"So sorry," he says, scrunching down as if pulling into a turtle shell. "I'll let you two deliberate longer."

"Wise choice." The Wise Woman stands, waving him away. She walks over to Audra, pulls her back up to sitting position, whispering fiercely, "Don't embarrass us, Audrey! These people need you to be your best self."

Audra nods, clutching her favorite book so tightly she bends the hardcover. She turns to the line and nods to the next two in line: the Jellyfish Girl and her twin. They step forward.

The girl on the left, most likely Nelly, speaks, "Good morning, Odd."

"—Drrraaaaaaaaaaaaaaa," Audra sighs.

The Jellyfish twins look at each other, shrug

their shoulders, and Nelly continues. "We thought we'd only see the old Wise Woman here. She's been encouraging me in my dream of becoming a costume designer."

"We're currently tightrope walkers and synchronized swimmers," Shelly adds.

"But now we're so glad to see you here as well, Odd, because we want you to be my first inspiration. I'm sure I could design you something much more dazzling than those plain clothes you have on. So how about it?"

Audra doesn't answer. She doesn't want to be rude, but playing dress-up never was her favorite game. It was Natalia's. She looks at them and smiles awkwardly.

After a long silence, Shelly says, "I want to be a firebreather, so any advice for that would be great!"

During another long pause, Audra searches her mind for an answer, but firebreathing sounds like such a dangerous profession that the only advice she can think of is: "Uhhh...practice?"

Slightly bewildered, the twins look to the Wise Woman, who smiles and waves for them to move on.

Audra also looks at the Wise Woman. Audra gestures to her wristwatch and pantomimes a cup of tea, hoping for a break. The Wise Woman shakes her head and gestures to the line.

Audra sighs as the next girl steps forward.

"Look at my new talent," this tiger-striped girl says as she bends backward and keeps on bending until she can crawl through her own legs.

Audra gapes, wide-eyed, as the tiger girl continues to twist, contort, and balance in impossible shapes. Finally, the girl ends in a normal standing position and bows.

Audra claps, squeamish but impressed.

"I've taught my macaw parrot seven new words," says a guy resembling a rabbit. He holds out his arm and a blue parrot flies down and lands there.

"Birds," Audra says to herself. That gives her an idea, "That would solve your food problem. Why don't they eat the birds?"

Everyone around her gasps and the Wise Woman sits up straight. “We aren’t savages. Birds are sacred.”

“They are?” Audra asks, face blushing.

“No more requests for wisdom, today,” the Wise Woman tells the onlookers. “Let’s see the rest of your tricks.

Audra sinks into her pillow. With every trick, she grows more fascinated. She is astonished when a tall, lanky man draws a smiley face in disappearing ink and lights it on fire to reveal a portrait of the Ringmaster. She cheers at the gripping performance where an archer shoots an apple out of someone’s hand. She laughs at the clowns as they mourn the death of their balloon. Audra claps louder and louder, forgetting her timidity for a long moment.

The jubilance fades from her face, however, at sight of a mother, father, and their daughter who step forward from the line. Though they are dressed as colorful feathered birds, their faces project a deep sense of grief. The father stands tall, silently watching and waiting. The mother gestures for the girl to move forward. Their child obeys and takes

five steps forward, holding her tightly-wrapped, trembling arm in a sling.

"Good morning, Wise One," the young girl says timidly.

"Good morning," Audra whispers, moved with compassion for this injured young girl.

The father stays behind while the mother walks forward. "We hope that with all of your knowledge," the mother says, struggling to hold back tears, "that you could help our daughter. She cut her arm last week and the infection is getting worse every day."

Audra's heart aches. If only she were a doctor or a nurse. She did have a medical book at her new home. And a trip home would undoubtedly give her some time for some peace and quiet. What a wonderful idea!

"Of course I will help!" Audra leaps to her feet.

The Wise Woman, who had dozed off, awakens with a disoriented stare.

"Just wait for me here while I go find the book you'll need," Audra says, leaving immediately.

The mother looks to the father.

"I'll stay here and wait," the father says with a strong, determined look in his eyes. "You can take her home to rest." The mother nods and takes the girl in her arms and heads right, toward her home. The father turns left and sits on a nearby wall, staring in the direction Audra went.

Turning back only to see the father waiting, Audra strides out of the village, walking home with a sense of purpose and determination. As she walks past a group of conversing men, her posture slumps inward. She clutches her dress nervously.

"Hey wait up a second," says one of them, "aren't you the new Wise One?"

"Yes, but I'm on an errand," Audra replies, quickening her pace.

"We need your opinion for a second," another man says, running up and stopping her from behind. He pushes her toward the group.

"I need to ..." Audra starts to say, but then trails off as her confidence falters, "Please, I..."

"We need to settle our discussion," says a large, gruff fellow sharpening his spear. Another man reaches out to put Audra into the center of their group.

"You know what!" says Audra, upset. "How about you settle something for me? All I want is peace and quiet. That's all I've wanted for most of my life. This island was supposed to bring me solace. But everywhere I turn, some needy person is begging me for attention. Why do you need my help? Can't you sit down and talk it out and learn to get along? Can't you let a lady have one moment of peace?"

The men back away throughout Audra's tempered rant.

"Audra?" Penny Peacock calls out, staring in through the gap in the group.

"Penny!" Audra jumps away from the group and takes her friend by the arm. "I need to talk to you."

Audra pulls Penny along for a rapid stroll through the forest.

The men watch the ladies for a few moments, then turn back to their discussion.

For a few moments, Audra and Penny walk in

peace. A small breeze dances its way through the trees and vegetation. The sunlight decorates the forest in patchy patterns of light. Distant wildlife sounds create a delightful ambiance. Audra looks over at Penny, who smiles.

"I'm so glad you came, Penny." Audra sighs in relief. "Sometimes I wish I were a completely different person. I feel like a little sardine in a sea of a hundred sharks."

Penny smiles, "Well, you were pretty bold with those men. I hardly recognized you."

Audra laughs, "Right. But now I can get some alone time and calm down."

Penny looks away, silent.

Audra then realizes she had forgotten she had planned to listen to Penny first thing, and she can see by her reaction that Penny may have been hoping for the same thing.

"After we talk, of course," Audra adds.

Penny smiles and gestures as if she is about to speak, but she is interrupted by a loud explosion coming from the ocean.

Birds flee upward and small animals scatter

further into the forest depths. Penny's face fills with deep concern. She turns toward the ocean.

"What was that?" Audra wonders out loud.

"Come with me!" Penny interrupts, bolting away toward the beach. Audra follows, running at a full sprint through the forest growth. Her hand loses its clutch on her *Circus Elephant* book. It slips out of her hands and falls to the forest floor.

"Wait," Audra hollers as she backtracks and plucks up the book. She catches up to Penny and runs beside her.

At last, they come to a boulder at the edge of the forest.

Penny ducks behind the boulder.

Audra follows.

"Please be careful," Penny whispers, "the Ring-master doesn't want these outsiders to spot us."

Audra rolls her eyes. "Of course he doesn't."

"Shhh," says Penny, ducking down.

Chapter 10: Dynamite

With her back against the cold slab of stone, Audra waits, watching Penny as she peeks out to the ocean. Quickly returning to hiding, Penny waits a few breaths and then peeks out again. This time, she spies a little longer, holding out her hand, signaling for Audra to be still.

"What are we looking at?" says Imaginary-Kendra from a puff of aqua-blue smoke on Audra's shoulder.

"SHHHH!" Audra responds.

Penny looks at Audra, puzzled. Audra smiles sheepishly. Penny turns back.

They wait.

They listen.

They wonder.

"Okay!" Penny finally motions for Audra to join her in peeking over the boulder. "They've finally gone inside their boat. Duck if you see them come out."

Audra creeps up from behind the boulder to see a red fishing boat out in the ocean. "Hmm," she exhales, "I thought I was crazy the first time I saw … wait … that symbol." At sight of a familiar, white symbol painted onto the side of the boat, Audra goes into deep thought. She's seen that symbol somewhere before.

"Get down," Penny urgently whispers as she pulls Audra down with her.

Penny breathes heavily, her hand holding her pounding heart. Audra turns toward Penny with an ever-distant stare. "I think I know where I've seen it!"

"Those fishermen," Penny explains, "are going to destroy this island."

Audra imagines the fishermen close up, with dastardly mustaches and thick scowling brows, hiding in the shadows of their crusty fisherman's caps. As Penny continues her explanation, Audra's imagination moves under the ocean into a colorful, lively reef of fish and ocean life.

"They line our beautiful reef with dynamite. They blow it up, bit by bit, all to quickly fill their fishing nets. I was told that William was last seen approaching these men. I heard he pretended to be alone and stranded and they took him away on their boat." Penny's eyes well up with tears. "And when I heard that, I realized he had chosen to leave me ... leave us."

Audra's eyes dart all over the place as her mind connects the many things she's learned over the past couple of days.

"But I also realized that maybe these men aren't as bad as the Ringmaster suspects," Penny continues. "I want to honor the Ringmaster's wishes, but I worry that our time is running out, that maybe I do need to do something—"

"You CAN!" Audra shouts jumping to her feet. She grabs a very surprised Penny by the arm and hoists her up. They dash together through a hundred trees, onto the sandy beach, and up the vine-covered ramp to Audra's home. Audra bursts in through her door and runs toward a stack of papers. She rummages through them like an excited squirrel until she finds the deed to her island and the accompanying inspection report. And there it is, the same logo from the boat, stamped in red at the top.

"I knew it!" she shouts, skipping across the room to her bookshelf. Like a child in a toy store, she eagerly picks five books from various spots on the shelf, making delighted squeals at every selection. With those books in her arms, she springs back over to Penny, who is holding back a laugh with her hand.

"These four are for you," Audra says, handing Penny the whole stack. "And this medical book is for that bird family with the injured daughter," she says, placing the last book on top.

Silence.

Penny looks down at the books, "I'm sorry, I'm confused."

"You can solve any problem with the right

books!" Audra explains. "*The Scarlet Pimpernel, Charlotte's Web, Swiss Family Robinson, and Matilda*: they are all about difficult problems and the awesome plans the heroes use to conquer them! You have such a brilliant, engineering mind. I'm sure you can figure out how to stop the dynamite fishermen. YOU can be the one to save the island!"

Penny stares back, speechless, blinking.

"You can read, can't you?" Audra asks.

"Well yes," Penny nods, "but wouldn't it be easier if you just tell me what the books say? Then we could come up with a plan together."

"I'd love to help, but I have to figure out how to get my communication device back from the Ringmaster so I can get out of here."

Penny stares at Audra with great distress. "You mean you'd abandon us?"

"Well, no, not forever, I just need to ..." Audra starts. "It's just so uncouth of your Ringmaster to destroy my solace and steal my only means of communicating with the outside world."

"Why don't you just try and earn his trust?" asks Penny.

"He's a thief and a liar," Audra responds, "Shouldn't he be earning my trust?"

"He did save your life," Penny insists, "He just has a hard time trusting outsiders, that's all."

"Exactly. Why should I even try?" Audra sits down, frustrated. Both she and Penny think for a bit.

"Look," Penny says, handing the book from the top of her pile, "If I were you, I'd take this medical book and help that bird family, see if you can quickly help anyone else, and then ask all of us to return the favor and talk to the Ringmaster for you. He'll have to listen to a group of us."

Audra looks down at the medical book in her hands. Penny does have a great idea, and Audra had promised to help the family herself.

"Okay," Audra says as she rushes to the cupboard and retrieves a bottle of herbs and a small medical kit. She slips them into her pocket. "You come up with your plan, I'll work through mine, and then we'll meet here after sundown. Will that work?" Audra says, walking toward the door.

Penny follows, eyeing her intimidating book pile. "Sure, but I don't think I'll finish all of these books in time. I do have some other things to do. Can I just leave the books here and work on it?"

"Sure," Audra says gently.

"Great!" Penny tosses the books on the table right next to Audra's *Circus Elephant* book and runs out the door. "See ya later!"

Audra smiles and gently locks the door behind her, leaving *The Circus Elephant* on the table.

The sun surpasses its noonday position. Audra runs back through the forest toward the circus village. Once there, she slows down to a walk to catch her breath. She takes a few steps up the ramp, but at the sight of a group passing by, she rushes down the ramp and ducks behind a tree. Turning to the right, she walks the village perimeter looking inward until she spots a ramp no one is using. She tiptoes up that ramp and peeks down the walkway to the left. She then peeks down the walkway on the right. There she spots one of the Jellyfish Girls walking her way. Audra turns right around and flees a few steps down the ramp, but then her mind lights up with an idea.

"Psst," Audra says as the Jelly-Fish Girl passes.

The girl stops and turns toward Audra.

"Are you Nelly or Shelly?" Audra asks.

"Nelly," she responds, delighted, taking a few steps down the ramp.

"Oh good, do you still want to design a quick costume for me?"

"Do I ever!" Nelly grabs Audra by the hand and yanks her toward the city.

"Wait," Audra shouts, and then quietly asks, "Can we go around the outside as much as possible?"

"Sure!" Nelly circles around, yanks her down the

ramp and before they know it, they run in through the backdoor of Nelly and Shelly's treehouse.

"Ahahaha!" Shelly shouts when Audra and Nelly enter. "I don't know how you convinced her, but this is going to be fun!"

"Can you do it in less than 10 minutes?" Audra asks, timidly.

"Of course," Nelly and Shelly reply in unison.

Shelly tosses Audra into a rusted barber chair while Nelly pulls out her measuring tape. Nelly holds the measuring tape up to various locations on Audra's body and shouts the measurements while Shelly takes notes. They toss various fabrics, ribbons, tassels, and buttons around Audra, checking how certain colors go with her skin tone, running back and forth from an old sewing machine. Finally, they pull Audra, fully dressed in her elephant-inspired costume, over to a full-length mirror.

Audra gasps, "I don't even…" She pulls at the different pieces of fabric, looking from the mirror to the girls to the fabric to the mirror. She trembles, teetering between nervousness and delight.

"A completely different woman, right?" Nelly claps enthusiastically.

Penny Peacock bursts in through the front door. "Shelly! Nelly! I've come up with a plan to beat the fishermen and I need your help." Penny glances over at a disguised Audra, thinks for a second, and looks back to the Jellyfish twins, "Do you have time?"

Audra quickly says, "Thank you," and hurries out the open front door.

Penny pauses for a moment and looks from Nelly to Shelly to Nelly to Shelly.

"Wait, was that...?" she asks. The sisters look at each other and giggle.

In the midday sun, Audra rushes down the ramps. Unrecognized by all she passes, her stride grows more and more confident. She gradually makes her way to the spot where the concerned father still waits for her. When she reaches him she finds him dozed off, sleeping while sitting. Audra stands in front of him, hesitating, reaching out, hesitating, reaching further, pulling back. After a few minutes of debate, she winces, bites her lip, and touches his shoulder.

"HUH?" The father jumps as he wakes.

"Sorry!" Audra jumps too.

"Oh," The father catches his breath. He peers at her in her new costume. "Sorry. Late night. I see you brought the book!"

"Yes!" Audra smiles awkwardly, extending the book toward him, nodding her head. "Yes...yes."

She hands the medical book to the father.

"Thank you!" The father's hands tremble as he tightly clutches the book. He gives a little bow then turns away to hurry home.

Audra watches him with smiling eyes, and just as he nearly leaves her sight, she shouts. "Oh!" She reaches into her pocket and pulls out the small medical kid and the bottle of herbs. "I forgot!" She runs after him, turning the same corner he just turned only to see him go around another. She runs around that corner to see him enter his own front door.

"The herbs!" Audra says, following the father in through the door. "You'll need these!" Audra stands near the doorway, catching her breath. The father receives the herb bottle with a grateful nod.

He is in such a hurry that he runs, lands on his knees, and slides to the bedside.

Audra looks around the humble dwelling. This treehouse has only one room. The mother sits by their daughter's bed at the back of the house. The girl looks over at Audra with tears in her eyes, which gush freely as her father unpins her bandage. She sucks her other thumb for comfort. The mother opens the book at the bookmark and scours the page to discover the remedy.

Red and swollen, with dark patches of infection, the young girl's arm trembles as her father slowly peels the bandage away from the skin.

Audra turns away, tossing away the tears from her own eyes. She walks out the open front door. If she had her favorite book she would have hugged it tight, but she has nothing to hug but herself, so she does. She takes a seat on a nearby bench, looking up at the sky through an opening in the forest canopy. Every time she glances back to see that humble family through the window, tears again grace her cheeks in wet streaks.

After a half hour, Audra starts to feel like she should be doing something to help. She takes one of the 10 empty cans there and fills it with flowers to bring some needed cheer to the room. Then she returns to her bench and watches and waits.

The afternoon passes like a sunny blur. Later that evening, the girl begs her father for some food. "So...hungry," she mutters weakly. The father checks the cans for food and finding them empty he returns to her bed with a reassuring smile. "I will find some food tomorrow," he says hopefully.

The girl rolls over, holding her stomach.

Tears return to Audra's cheeks. She closes her eyes and clasps her hands so tightly that her whole body shakes. Then her eyes pop open with a fire of purpose. She hops up and bolts back to the path she had run to come here before: to the left around a corner, a couple wrong turns, several steps of back-tracking, to the right around another corner, up the staircase, and through the door of the Ringmaster's quarters.

"I'm ready!" she announces.

Startled, the Ringmaster turns and knocks his bowl of soup on the floor. "Augh!" He grumbles, looking from the mess to Audra. "Nice costume, Odd."

Audra continues, "I'm ready to take you up on your offer."

The Ringmaster stares at her, studies her, and says, "Really? What made you change your mind?"

"I've decided I do care about your people. I want to help." Audra replies, fidgeting nervously, hoping the Ringmaster will actually believe her and not start up another argument.

"Interesting," he says, scrubbing the floor on his hands and knees. "You know, I've been watching you since you got here. And I think you don't care about anybody but yourself. So how do I know I can trust you?"

"TRUST? YOU don't trust ME?" Audra mutters to herself, turning away. She quickly turns back, "You know, not everyone is a crooked schemer like you."

"And is that any way to speak to the man who saved your life?" the Ringmaster asks, getting in her face.

"Oh, I have a theory about that," Audra retorts.

"Hit me with it," the Ringmaster seethes.

Audra backs away from the Ringmaster, suddenly very self-conscious and feeling a bit guilty for her foolish words.

"Go on, tell me." The Ringmaster forces a smile. "I can take it."

"Oh it's pretty silly," says Audra, twiddling her fingers.

The Ringmaster waits, his arms folding. Audra feels even more awkward.

"I just imagined," Audra says, "that you sent the tiger and staged the rescue to win my trust."

The Ringmaster tightens his folded arms. He grits his teeth. "You also thought I banished Penny's husband and caused him to leave the island."

"How did you know that?" Audra asks.

"Penny came to me with a couple new questions about the night he came to see me," the Ringmaster blurts out. "What other crazy rumors have you concocted? Maybe you're the crooked schemer after all!"

Audra stares at him, bewildered. She can't believe he would make that kind of accusation about her, a sweet and quiet woman.

An interrupting bugle sounds in the distance. The Ringmaster jumps up, grabs a fancy coat and whips right out the door.

"I have to go," he shouts back.

"Oh no you don't," Audra grumbles, chasing him.

Chapter 11: History And Stardom

The Ringmaster sprints forward. As Audra follows behind, the running gap between them grows. In the midst of intersecting walkways, crowds of people block Audra's path and she loses complete sight of the Ringmaster. Dashing through every opening in the crowd, she quickly becomes disoriented. Looking right while running left, she runs straight into someone's outstretched arms.

Those arms wrap around her and she hears a familiar voice, "Calm yourself, little elephant."

Audra looks up to see the Wise Woman's smiling face.

"Are you running toward something or away?" the Wise Woman asks.

"That charlatan! That..." Audra shouts, out of breath, "He just ... and I ... and then he ...ugh."

"The Ringmaster?" The Wise Woman asks, with a patient smile.

Audra nods her head.

"You don't like him, do you?" the Wise Woman observes. "Yet strangely enough, everyone else around here loves him."

"Loves him?" Audra asks, surprised by the word choice. The Wise Woman puts her arm around Audra.

"Yes," the Wise Woman says, "and if you took the time to get to know him, you'd find a man who has saved not only your life but the lives of many."

Audra becomes even more confused. "Why don't I trust him then?" She asks, "Why is there something deep down that tells me that with every good I hear about him, there's something nefarious hidden beneath?"

"Here's what we'll do..." says the Wise Woman. "You'll close your eyes and I'll tell you a story. You'll trust me as we walk, I won't let you run into anything."

Audra looks at her for a moment, blinking in deliberation. "Like a trust exercise?"

"Heaven knows you need one," the Wise Woman replies.

Audra sighs and closes her eyes.

The Wise Woman leads her forward by the shoulders, calmly revealing her tale: "Thirty years ago, Patrick dreamed he would become the Ringmaster of the greatest circus the world had ever seen. We all believed he would be, but while some audiences applauded our performances, other audiences booed and even threw half-eaten food at our sour acts. Patrick would try to lighten the mood by tasting the food and shouting back, "Delicious! Thanks!"

Every word from the Wise Woman becomes a new image in Audra's imagination. She sees an audience booing the young Ringmaster, throwing food to force him off the stage. He catches one of the sausages and happily takes a bite.

"His attitude always impressed me," the Wise Woman continues. "But I could see it wearing on him. In our traveling circus, everyone had to work from the moment we awoke to the instant we crashed on our hay-stuffed pillows. We usually slept on the train. We'd arrive, set up the tents, the stands, the lights. We'd care for the animals, we'd dress, perform, run the lights, calm the animals, crash to our straw beds, wake up, clean the animals, risk our necks performing again, take down the circus, pack it away, sleep on the bumpy road, and do it all again.

"One day, I noticed Patrick had stopped working. He was looking around at his people. He watched them, straining, weak, their backs cracking, their feet dragging. He visibly broke down for a moment, tears welling up in his eyes, then turned and rushed away. I found him behind one of our rusty train cars, sobbing like a big toddler. I hugged him something fierce, and we both cried together...

"'What are we doing this for?' he asked.

"I answered, 'We love the spotlight.'

"Then he said, 'So why don't we just get rid of everything else and just perform for the spotlight?' And we both kind of chuckled at that, but then that idea stuck in his noggin. I'd see him awake while most were sleeping, reading and scribbling by the light of streetlamps.

"He came up with a crazy plan to ship us all from Europe to America. He figured we just needed a new kind of audience. He was certain American audiences would be more generous. He convinced the whole crew that it was a good idea. And we were all so excited until the storm came. When the ship hit a rock, I was sure our lives were over, but Patrick was too much of a hero to let that happen. He led a heroic rescue, saving others who couldn't swim, inspiring others to help. He shouted and cheered for us until his voice went hoarse. The next morning, he gave a stirring speech inspiring us to build this community, continue to practice our circus skills, and he often joked that we finally found a way to enjoy the circus without the daily strain."

"And you're sure he didn't crash the boat on purpose?" Audra blurts out. Then feeling guilty of making such an accusation, she covers her mouth. "Sorry."

"Calm down, cherry blossom." The Wise Woman massages Audra's shoulders. "You have reason to mistrust him. He has honestly botched every interaction you two have had. But he was only hiding your home so the fishermen wouldn't see it. Years ago, when the fishermen first arrived, they were exploring the island, searching for treasure. The Ringmaster took some men to meet them, and a fight broke out."

"No surprise there," Audra mutters under her breath, her eyes still closed.

"The Ringmaster," the Wise Woman continues, "is a peaceful man unless provoked. The fishermen started the fight. Our men fiercely defended themselves. Finally, they held the fishermen cornered at spearpoint. The Ringmaster made them promise to leave the island forever. They begged for a compromise. They wanted permission to fish the reef as long as they promised never again to set foot on the island. The Ringmaster refused to agree to that. But that's when an unforeseen fisherman appeared with a gun to Andrew's head—"

"Tiger boy?" Audra asked intently.

"He had followed them there. And Patrick wasn't about to let his son die that day. So he agreed to a compromise. The man lowered his gun and they shook on it, but just before they left the gunman threatened, 'If we ever see any of your people again, even on the beach, we will not lower our guns again.'

"So that's the reason for the Ringmaster's rules. When they fish on one side of the island, we fish on the other. When a woman builds a home on the beach, we camouflage it. If you think about it, that's one more time he saved your life."

"Wow," Audra says. This story was completely different from what she had imagined. The Ringmaster was not the villain, after all.

But there was one thing that still didn't make

sense. "Wait, how did William approach the fishermen without getting shot?"

"He pretended to drown and for some reason, they rescued him," the Wise Woman says, thoughtfully. "I was happy to see there was some goodness in them."

"Audra!" comes Penny Peacock's familiar voice.

Finally opening her eyes, Audra finds herself in what looks like the backstage wing of a theater. Music, ringing bells, and cheering sound in the distance. She spots Penny running toward her.

"It's all ready!" Penny gleams. "I just drew up the final plan."

"Really?" Audra says with both joyful surprise and a tinge of nervousness. "Show me."

Penny unrolls a stack of large papers with schematics for boats.

"How long will these take to build?" Audra asks.

"Built! I've been working on them for years." Penny says in a giddy tone. "And here's the battle plan." She shows Audra the last sheet.

Audra only looks at the plan for a moment, when her mind lights up with an idea. "This is great, but let me suggest..." Audra looks at the Wise

Woman and fearing too much input from other sources, whispers in Penny's ear.

"That many?" Penny asks with an expression of surprise.

"Am I changing your plan too much?" Audra asks.

"Not if you think it will work," Penny replies.

"I'm sure of it," Audra responds.

"Well, I gue—uuugh..." Before Penny can complete her sentence, she cringes in pain and holds her stomach.

"Penny?" Audra backs away, struggling to think of what to do to help.

Penny's face relaxes. "I'm fine," she says, breathing heavily. "This happens every so often."

Shelly pops in from the backstage curtain. She shouts, "Penny, you're on!"

"Oh, right. I'm on," Penny says, recovered from

the pain, hurrying to the curtain. "Break a leg, Audra!"

Penny parts the curtains and walks into the colorful burst of light.

"Wait..." Audra mutters, confused, "Why did she tell me to..."

The Wise Woman responds, strangely nervous, "Audra, how about another trust exercise?"

"Well," Audra answers, hesitant. "I don't know. Maybe..."

"Great! Once you get past the nerves, you're going to love this." The Wise Woman gestures toward the curtain.

"Wait!" Audra squeaks.

Four hands seize Audra from behind. Two burly men raise Audra above their heads and carry her through the curtains. Bright stage lights (made from a combination of lanterns and mirrors) shine directly in Audra's eyes. The audience applauds and cheers as flashes of colored ribbons soar around her. She looks around the circus ring and spots Penny in the brightest area of light.

Balancing atop a multi-colored ball, Penny performs a strange dance while the audience sings "la la las" in what sounds like a lullaby. Her dance consists of swinging her peacock tail around, massaging her stomach with both hands, and singing at the top of her lungs, eyes closed. Audra notices that she is part of a procession of people circling Penny. Some are dancing and some are blowing kisses.

With one eyebrow raised and the other eye squinted, Audra studies the scene with deep perplexity. Between the flashing colors, the lovely melody, and the odd sincerity of their actions, the act is simultaneously beautiful and unnerving.

The two men carrying Audra set her next to Penny's ball. As Audra looks up at Penny sparkling in the limelight, her perplexed expression transforms into awe and admiration. Penny opens her eyes, bows to the audience's applause, and glances mid-bow to Audra. With elegant grace, Penny slides down the ball and gives Audra a back pat.

"Now it's your turn," Penny whispers.

Audra immediately slips away from Penny and backs away in terror.

Penny gently catches her and places both hands on her shoulders. She speaks loudly as to be heard over the buzzing crowd. "You are in costume, remember? You could be as crazy as you are able and you'd look absolutely typical. Show everyone you are one of us now."

Audra relaxes a bit.

Penny continues, "And it doesn't matter what you do, they'll still clap for you. I promise."

Slowly, Penny removes one hand from Audra's shoulder and pats her on the back while carefully turning Audra toward the audience with her other hand. Like a sloth leaving her baby, Penny takes one step away, then another. Audra notices the other circus performers slipping away. She looks behind her just in time to see Penny disappear behind the curtains. Because the bright lights and dusty air hide her view of the audience, it appears as if she is entirely alone. The audience, with all eyes on Audra, stops talking. Only jungle sounds remain.

Stillness, the moon overhead, settling dust, bright lights, and a sea of barely visible faces wait for Audra. Her heart still pounds, her breath still accelerates, her knees tremble, her eyes flutter, her body starts to teeter. As Audra widens her stance and tries to keep her composure, an Imaginary-Kendra and Natalia peek out from their hiding places in Audra's costume.

"I know I'm always saying advance," Imaginary-Kendra says, "but tonight I'm saying RETREAT!" Audra looks down to see her usually tough sister trembling from stage fright.

"Odd! Odd! Odd! Odd!" The audience starts chanting.

"Why not enjoy the glamorous spotlight?" Natalia counters, "Sing a little song! You'd look much more foolish by running away."

"Odd! Odd! Odd! Odd!" the audience continues.

Audra looks to the backstage curtain, to the audience, to a trembling Kendra, and to a light-basking Natalia.

"Odd! Odd! Odd! Odd!"

Well, she might as well start by setting her name straight. Audra squares her shoulders and fully faces the audience.

"It's AUDRAAAA," she shouts!

The crowd goes silent. All of the immediate attention only increases Auda's nervous state.

"My name," Audra squeaks, "is Audra."

"Say hi to Audra," Penny shouts out.

The crowd shouts in unison, "Hi Audra!"

Penny motions to Audra to go on. Audra takes a deep breath. The sooner she does this, the sooner it will be over, right? Too bad the last time she sang in front of anyone was in the 3rd grade. She clasps both hands together, brings her shoulders back in for security and opens her mouth. But fear holds her voice hostage and all she feels she can do is nervously shake her head.

An unexpected hand clasps Audra's trembling fingers. Penny gives her a reassuring smile and proceeds to sing with the familiar actions:

I'm a little teapot
Short and stout

Penny gestures for Audra to continue the song. Audra lets out her long-held breath, followed by a giggle. Penny continues singing and Audra joins in with the tiniest hand gestures she can muster:

Here is my handle
Here is my spout

Audra's volume increases just as Penny drops out. Penny flashes Audra a smile and continues the silly actions as Audra sings solo:

When I get all steamed up
Hear me SHOUT!

Audra covers her mouth and giggles, then continues in a full, beautiful voice:

Tip me over and
Pour...
Me...
Out...

The audience applauds generously. Audra's face flushes red. "I can't believe I did that."

"Welcome to the circus," shouts one male voice from the crowd.

Penny takes Audra's hand and together they bow.

For the first time in her life, Audra enjoys a crowd's attention. As Penny gives her a bear hug — the first hug Audra has received since the death of her parents — tears well up in Audra's smiling eyes and trickle down through the corners of her smile. If only such a hug could last forever.

"See, that wasn't so bad," Penny smiles, ending the embrace.

"Well!" Audra responds, "I hope the Ringmaster saw that because I don't know if I can do it again."

Penny and Audra chuckle together.

"RINGMASTER!" screams a frantic male voice. The whole circus looks around for the source of the voice. The spotlight scans the crowd. Above the seats, a warrior-like man runs into the spotlight. "RINGMASTER!" the man screams again. "The monkeys are getting away with our supplies!"

A female warrior runs in from another direction. "The tigers are attacking and eating our fish

right at the riverside!"

With great concern, Audra runs up the steps, separate from the crowd to see if she can spot the Ringmaster. The spotlight moves from the warrior to her.

All eyes also turn to Audra, whose confidence suddenly retreats, replaced by panic. "What are you looking at me for? Where's the Ringmaster? Where's the Wise One?"

"You are the Wise One!" shouts another warrior-like man, coming up the stairs toward her. "When the Ringmaster is gone, we look to you!"

Chapter 12: Wisdom

Through the darkness of the forest, up one of the many circus walkways, a man runs about courageously, searching. His suit is tattered and muddy. His hair is unruly. The wind catches his untied tie and snatches it away into the air. "Audra?" he shouts. Hearing the sound of the buzzing circus crowd, he turns left and runs toward the lights. As he leaps out of the forest and into the light of the circus ring, he shouts one last time. "Audra?" One unfamiliar head in the crowd of circus people turns her head toward him.

"Norman?" Audra replies, surprised. This is the last place she expected to see her limousine driver.

"Audra!" Penny shouts, beckoning for her attention.

"Audra?" Norman squints, puzzled by Audra's new, unruly circus attire.

Penny grabs Audra's arm and leads her to higher ground.

Audra looks down at Norman. She would think his presence would make her nervous, but somehow he gives her strength. She shouts out, voice cracking, "Okay ... now ... who knows how to tame tigers?"

The warrior girl and guy jump forward, "We do, sir!"

Audra giggles as girlishly as she can. "Sir?"

"Yes, maam!" They shout in reply.

"Okay, you two tame the tiger ... and who knows how to catch monkeys?"

As the warriors run out, four new people raise their hands.

"Great," Audra says with a bit more gusto. "Hop to it!"

They obey.

"And Penny!" Audra shouts.

"Yes, Wise One," Penny says, hopping forward with a grin.

"While we have everyone gathered, let's put our plan in motion. Let's get this whole food shortage problem solved once and for all. Everyone else! Follow Penny."

"You heard her!" Penny shouts, running out, followed by several others.

"Except you, Norman!" Audra calls out, motioning for him to come over.

"I nearly searched the whole island looking for you," Norman says with a timid grin. "Christian Howard, your helicopter pilot, he called me and we thought you might need rescuing. Guess we were wrong, huh?"

"Oh no," Audra says, feeling most relieved. "I'm in definite need of a way home. Where's the pilot?"

"Oh," Norman replies, "Well he needed to help someone else, but he said you had a way to phone him once I found you."

Audra groans. This was not the news she was hoping for. But wait. She tells Norman her new idea. "Maybe we can find it while everyone else is busy!"

Norman has no chance to respond.

"Where is everybody?" the Ringmaster's voice calls out. "Audra?"

Audra turns to see the Ringmaster carrying the injured bird girl on his shoulder. Her noble parents walk out beside him.

"Well, Patrick," Audra says, "I've just set plans in motion that will solve all of your problems."

"Patrick!?" The Ringmaster does not seem impressed with the news. He returns the girl to her parents and stomps toward her. "No one sets plans in motion without my permission."

"Except the Wise Woman, of course," Audra says, standing her ground.

"Okay, O Wise One. Where is everybody and what are they up to?" The Ringmaster says, now towering over her.

Audra cowers. "Taming the tiger, catching monkeys, and preparing down on the beach."

“The beach?” The Ringmaster panics and bolts off in that direction.

“Wait! What about my device?” Audra chases the Ringmaster, while Norman chases Audra.

Zipping through the forest, they run past several groups of runners with torches. The warm light of the flames and the blue light of the moon elegantly light the forest like a fairytale adventure land. Small fireflies speckle the bushes and bounce off the runners in their passing by.

Down the hill, in a break in the trees, Audra and her fellow runners pass five villagers who’ve caught a tiger. With ropes, they strain to strap the viciously thrashing tiger to a tree. As Audra rushes past the next few trees, that group recedes from view.

Out onto the sandy beach, the three runners emerge. Several boats have left the shore and now sail toward a glimmer of light that twinkles in the darkness. Down in the shallows, Penny waits on the last boat.

“Penny Peacock!” the Ringmaster shouts. “What are you all doing? You call those boats in right now.”

"But Ringmaster," Penny starts.

"Rules are rules, Penny!" the Ringmaster says, firmly.

Penny pounds the boat with the bottom of her oar. "You don't even know what our plan is!"

"Right!" Audra adds.

"Quiet, you!" the Ringmaster shouts at Audra.

Audra folds her arms and gives him a look of disgust.

The Ringmaster focuses back on Penny, "I can't trust a plan until I know every detail!"

"Trust?" Audra shouts out, arms folded even more tightly.

"Quiet!" The Ringmaster shouts. "Call the whole thing off, Penny, or I'll get up there and signal them myself. You're this close to losing my trust."

"Trust?" Audra shouts, jumping up on the boat next to Penny, "Trust? Trust is your favorite word, isn't it? But I think you've forgotten what that word means. You think it means you have control, but it doesn't. Trust means you are willing to let go of control. It's a belief in the goodness in people. And it's about time you get back to trusting your people. Trust us to follow through with our plan! Trust that the fishermen might somehow change their minds. Trust me enough to give me back my device!"

"Fine then!" The Ringmaster throws his arms in the air. "Go ahead. I can't wait for you to get out there to find out how foolish you actually are. I'll be right here waiting when you get back!"

"Oh, we'll go all right!" Audra motions to Penny, who sets the sail. "But we don't plan to fail!"

"Fine!" yells the Ringmaster.

"Fine!" Penny and Audra yell together. With that, they turn toward the sea. They sail forward at full speed.

Back on the shore, the Ringmaster glances over at Norman and barks, "Who are you?"

The poor guy stiffens his already stiff posture, "Norman!"

"So what are you doing here?" the Ringmaster grunts, looking back to the sea.

"Being absolutely useless, apparently," says

Norman. "Wait! Audra was looking for a communication device. It's a bulky phone that connects to a satellite. You wouldn't know where that is, would you?"

The Ringmaster turns to him with an angry smile. "Why yes! I do. Come with me and I'll give it to you." The Ringmaster trudges through the sand, up toward the trees. "Then she can leave this island and let me lead my people in peace!"

"Okay," Norman says, awkwardly. He follows the Ringmaster, tripping after him, struggling to balance as every step sinks into the sand. When they step into the forest, the ground becomes much more solid and Norman is able to catch up with the Ringmaster.

From twenty feet ahead in the dark of the jungle, one of the circus warriors runs toward them.

"Tiger!" she screams. "Tiger! It escaped!"

The Ringmaster turns to Norman, pointing to the left, "Quick. Run that way!" The Ringmaster runs in the opposite direction. He runs a few steps and glances behind him.

Norman has not obeyed. He stands frozen in terror. The tiger bounds toward him, leaps and spreads its claws. The Ringmaster knocks Norman out of the way and faces the tiger head on.

Norman falls to the ground and looks behind him. The Ringmaster and tiger wrestle, hidden in the bushes.

Several shouts echo through the forest trees as several warriors with torches and spears run in to confront the tiger.

The Ringmaster let's out a pain-laden scream. His scream echoes out toward the sea.

From the boat, Audra looks toward land, startled, then back at Penny. "Did you hear that?"

Penny holds a finger to her mouth, signaling for silence. She scans the surrounding ocean and they wait.

Audra sits beside Penny and looks back toward land, wondering about the scream she just heard. She couldn't see whether Norman or the Ringmaster still wait on the shore. Hopefully, they are all right.

Penny doubles over in pain, wincing, and struggling to breathe.

Audra looks at her friend with concern. She puts her arms around Penny and leans in to whisper. "Penny?"

"I'm fine," Penny gasps. "Keep watching the sea."

Audra looks out to the sea, and Penny gains control over her breathing.

A little burst of light shines out from the distant darkness.

"That's the signal," Penny whispers as she quickly lights a lantern to send a flash of light of her own back into the darkness.

She pulls a rope to increase the size of the sail,

and again she doubles over in pain with shortness of breath.

Audra stands and grabs the sail so that Penny can have a break.

"Not now," Penny whispers, "don't come yet." She breathes deeply for a couple minutes, then pulls herself back to her feet. "Okay," she whispers to Audra, "hopefully that's the last one for a while."

Audra studies Penny, watching her carefully. She's very concerned about these recurring pains Penny keeps having. It almost seems like Penny is pregnant. But wouldn't Penny have told her about it? Did Penny tell her and she missed it?

"Here we are," Penny whispers, "this better work!"

Chapter 13: Dazzling Climax

All is quiet. Crickets softly chirp from their hiding place in the nooks of the towering rock. The ocean waves gently lap against the side of the large, rusty boat which is anchored fifteen feet from one of the island's surrounding mini-islands.

On the deck of this fishing boat, a man bounces his crossed feet at the end of his lounging chair. A hat covers his head and face. His hands lay on his lap. His fingers play an unknown tune on nonexistent piano keys.

Another man sits beside him, his bare feet hanging over the boat side. By the light of his battery-powered lantern, he whittles at a piece of wood. Every half a minute he spits a wad of juice from whatever he is chewing into the ocean.

Both men look like they've come out from a cave or mud pit: thick beards and mustaches, angular baggy clothes, streaks of dirt and grime all over them. In the corner of the boat, newly caught fish fill an enormous net, glistening wet in the shadows. The whole outfit smells like a can of sardines.

A faint female singing voice drifts in from a distance. The whittling fisherman drops his wood block into the water. The lounging fisherman lifts his hat and looks out at the sea, which flows away from them and toward the main island. Several rectangular shadows drift toward them. The singing stops. The men scramble to their feet.

With a thick French accent, the shorter whittler asks, "Zis isn't a dream … right, Pierre?"

"It could be," Pierre responds, in an equally thick French accent.

The singing starts again, so close it sounds like it's right behind the fishermen. They rush back on their teetering boat and look to the water to see a ripple at the point from where the noise had come.

The singing starts on the other side, this time from two female voices. The men scramble back, trying to be the first to see. The short whittler loses his balance and falls toward the water. Right when his bulbous nose comes within 2 inches of a Jellyfish Girl's nose, Pierre catches him by the back of the belt. Léo gasps, "Mermaids?"

"Come on, Léo," Pierre says, pulling him back up. "Give me chance wit' ze ladies."

Serenades warm the chilly air. The Jellyfish Girls swim in mirror image, swirling, twisting, and crossing, under the surface and then over again. Pierre and Léo lean toward them, swaying back and forth in a silly-grinned similar way, gawking intently at the swimming beauties.

From out of the darkness, Audra's amplified voice booms, "Ladies and fishermen..."

Léo's head pops up to see encroaching shadowy boats. Pierre's head follows. Subtle mist rolls in from behind. Lights spring out from the shadows and reveal several silhouettes rushing back and forth. The lights vanish.

"We are proud to present..." Audra's voice comes louder.

Like a blooming flower, decorative patterns drawn in glow-in-the-dark ink unfold from the shadowy boats. Fifty circus performers stacked several persons high work together to form this fantastic spectacle.

Audra finishes the announcement. "The Crawdad Circus!"

Léo looks puzzled toward Pierre, then turns to the crawdad logo on the wall beside him.

Bright flashing lights draw their attention back to the show.

Dazzling girls soar toward the boat, bright colored drapery streaming behind them. They chant, circling the wide-eyed fishermen, wrapping colorful fabric around their necks, tickling their beaming cheeks with beautiful silk.

"I always wanted to see circus!" Pierre cheers, back to back with Léo.

“Then why not join the circus?” says Penny, emerging from the troupe with a devious grin. Two massive men pick up the fishermen and place them on their shoulders. The fishermen gleefully relish the spectacular crowd, which surrounds them upon the circle of boats.

The mime-faced turtle-ish man pops out from the crowd, juggling fish. He tosses two of the fish for the men to catch, but Léo misses, and Pierre gets a fish in the face. Both applaud and cheer, laughing as the juggler bows away.

Contortionists stack up, upheld by the swirling crowd. As they flex and form into each impossible pose, the fishermen gasp, gulp, shriek, whistle.

“Over here!” Nelly draws their attention to the left with a flirty finger wave. They turn to witness her blowing fire from her lips. She grins with sooty teeth as the fishermen cheerfully hoot and holler.

Act after act, a swirl of patterns: Purple, pink, orange, green, blue, yellow, red, chartreuse. The men cheer and jeer until their energy fades, worn down into a happy, smiling stupor.

Léo turns to Pierre just in time to see his smile disappear. Utterly bewildered, Pierre stares at Léo’s legs, then at his own. “Wait! What? What?” Léo whimpers. Unwittingly tied up by the circus performers, the fishermen look down to see the Brazilian zebra lady carrying them toward the dark door in the deck of Penny’s boat.

“Hey, what is zis?” Léo whines.

“Stop, let us go!” Pierre growls.

The Brazilian zebra woman calmly throws them into the base of the boat, She shuts the door, sealing the darkness. The entire crowd cheers.

“We did it,” Audra shouts, giddily shaking Penny by the arm, “Now we can lock them in my white box until we find a way to ship them out.”

Backpatting, clapping, and high-fiving abounds. Penny hugs Audra; the old Wise Woman hugs Penny, the turtle juggler embraces them all. One by one, all the circus performers join the group hug. At first, Audra tenses up and can’t wait for the embrace to end, but when she notices their happy smiles, their warm sparkling eyes, her muscles relax. And just as her smile joins theirs and she nuzzles into the embrace, the whole group releases their hug. They quickly tense up and face something behind Audra.

She turns and looks the same direction to see three men standing with guns pointed in her direction. She and the others had been so wrapped up in their activities that they hadn't even noticed this new fishing boat approaching.

"I thought there were only two fishermen, maybe three," Audra whispers to Penny.

"I wasn't sure how many there were," Penny whispers back.

"Release our men at once," commands the short man with the middle gun.

"They were trespassing on my island," Audra speaks out.

"I'm not going to ask twice," the short man shouts. He fires a shot in the air. At that signal, a giant tanker lights up 50 feet behind him. Countless men yell indistinguishable calls from the deck of that ship.

Audra, finally understanding the fear the people feel toward these fishermen, backs up and shuts her lips tight.

"Com certeza," says the Brazilian Zebra Lady. She immediately opens the door.

Léo and Pierre scramble out and leap over onto

the other fishing boat. “Thanks, boss,” they clamor together.

“Don’t we have guns?” Audra whispers to Penny.

“No,” Penny responds.

“Is there any chance they might attack the island now?”

Penny doesn’t answer vocally. She merely looks up with terror in her eyes.

And in terror, they wait while the three men with guns continue standing with their weapons pointed.

“One question,” says the boss. “What makes you think you own this island?”

“I bought it,” Audra says timidly, “from the bank. Your symbol was stamped on the inspection papers.”

The boss glares over at Léo and Pierre. “You declared the island UN-inhabited?”

“Yes, sir,” says Pierre with a smile. “We say no one live here.”

“You ffffffoools,” the boss seethes, “I told you to say no one COULD live here!”

“Yes!” Pierre says, smiling. “No one live here!”

The boss groans for a moment, but then his

groan becomes a chuckle, "Well Pierre, you just made me a wealthy man." He turns back to Audra, "Well, ma'am, sorry about the misunderstanding. Let us fish for one more day, and we'll leave your island."

"Really," Audra blurts out, surprised.

"Yep," he responds. "Of course it will be a BIG day of fishing. The reef will be destroyed, and you will have to leave soon after us. But that's the cost of doing business, 'innit?"

The other men laugh.

Audra and the circus people don't.

"And what if I don't agree?" asks Audra.

"It's non-negotiable," the boss responds, waving his gun around as a reminder. "Take us out boys," he calls out. Their boat motors away. The other fishing boat follows.

"Have a nice night," the boss calls out. All of the men laugh.

The circus people stay still, watching the men until they disappear into the night.

When the coast is clear, they all solemnly disperse to their boats, set their sails, and slowly return to the beach. With heavy hearts and no

words, they carry their boats, climb the beach, and disappear into the jungle.

All alone, ten paces below Audra's beach home, Penny and Audra sit down in the sand and stare out at the ocean. The relaxing sound of the waves calms the bitterness of their defeat. Every so often, Audra shakes her head and sighs. Penny glances at Audra often, then she turns to the ocean, then back to Audra.

"Audra," Penny whispers after quite some time. "Would you mind if I stayed in your house tonight?"

Audra keeps her eyes on the ocean. "Of course," she answers. "Go ahead and use the bed."

"Won't you need it?" Penny asks, standing up with a groan.

"No," Audra responds. There's no way she could sleep tonight.

"Okay," Penny says, trudging away.

Audra goes back into her silence, her mind heavy from the events of the night. The Ringmaster was correct; she was a fool. And now because of her ridiculous plan, the island reef would soon be destroyed.

Over and over in her mind, she repeats the events of the night: her run-ins with the Ringmaster, the thrilling performance, the applause of the audience, the unexpected hugs, the capture of the fishermen, the fired gunshot, the mocking tone of the short-statured boss.

"You don't understand people," Imaginary-Kendra puffs up on Audra's shoulder.

"Do you?" Imaginary-Natalia punctuates the criticism from the other shoulder.

Audra continues her unbroken ocean gaze. She stares at the ocean nearly the entire night, at least it feels like the entire night. Her eyes finally grow heavy and she closes them for what she thinks will be only a moment, but when the sound of an explosion wakes her up, she opens her eyes to see the morning.

More explosions follow.

Silhouetted in the light of a brilliant sunrise, an enormous tanker casts a long shadow that reaches just beyond Audra. From that shadow, she watches as at least a dozen fishing boats swarm about, setting off explosions and casting nets to boatloads of fish.

Though the view is painful for Audra to watch, she forces herself to keep watching. She must face the consequences of her actions. She's been trying to escape reality for so long that she had almost forgotten the difference between fantasy and real life. Reality, especially today, was ugly.

She continues to watch until the sun has fully risen, until a desperate scream comes from Audra's home.

She finally breaks her ocean watch to look behind her.

The scream comes again, and Audra knows whose it is.

"Penny!"

Chapter 14: Unexpected Climax

Audra stumbles through the sand, rushes up her ramp, rips the door open and stares in from the doorway.

"It's coming," Penny howls, writhing on the bed. "I think my water just broke!"

"So you ARE pregnant!" Audra shouts, half surprised and half excited. "I was starting to wonder, but I didn't want to be presumptuous."

"I told you," Penny says, breathing heavily. "But I wasn't sure if you were listening."

"Nope," Imaginary-Natalia says, puffing out on Audra's shoulder. "She must have been in one of her dazes."

"She misses a lot," Imaginary-Kendra adds.

Audra sighs, annoyed by her imaginary sisters.

"Audra!" shouts the distant, very real voice of Norman. He runs up the ramp and in the open door. Out of breath, he struggles. "The Ringmaster...attacked...by a tiger...he asked to see you...at once...he's dying."

Audra groans. Everything seems to be going wrong at once.

Penny howls out again as another contraction grows in intensity.

Norman looks from Audra to Penny to Audra, "Is she?"

"Help!" Audra nods. "We need help."

"Oh, m-my..." Norman stutters. "R-Right, I'll grab some help." He runs out the door. "I'll be right back." He shuts the front door and runs down the ramp.

Audra stands, feeling helpless, watching Penny from afar.

"Well, don't just stand here," Imaginary-Kendra blurts, still standing on Audra's shoulder.

"I've never even seen a baby delivered," Audra whispers petrified. "What if I mess it up?"

"Wouldn't surprise us," Imaginary-Natalia snickers.

"Buzz off, Natalia!" says Imaginary-Kendra. "Don't you have a medical book on this?"

"The book!" Audra shouts, frantically searching her bookshelf, pulling books off and flinging them behind her. "Where is it? I know I saw it somewhere..."

"You mean the book you gave to the little girl's family?" Imaginary-Kendra asks.

"No, I'm sure that was a different one," Audra says, checking the pile of books a second time. "At least," she stops. "No, you're right."

Penny groans, breathing hard.

"Hang in there," Audra shouts, running toward the door. She trips and catches herself by grabbing the doorknob.

Imaginary-Natalia, standing on Audra's hand on the doorknob, stares down at her sternly. "You can't leave her here all alone."

"Right!" Imaginary-Kendra chimes in. "Books aren't the answer to every problem."

Imaginary-Natalia adds, "Stop being a scaredy cat, Audra!"

"Fine!" Audra stands in anger. "You're right!"

"What?" her shoulder sisters react in unison.

"You're right that I'm plain. You're right that I'm not tough enough. You're right that I'm childish. You're right that I'm a scaredy cat. Why else would I waste millions on my own private island?

"But here is where you were wrong: You were wrong to tell me that no one would like me. That I couldn't have friends. That I would never be happy until I was alone."

Clap, Clap, Clap, Clap. With a huge grin, Kendra applauds Audra's words.

"Keep going, Audra," Natalia cheers with a proud expression. "Let Kendra have it!"

"She was talking to you too!" Kendra snaps back.

"I'd love to keep going," Audra answers, walking

toward Penny as her two imaginaries float behind her. "But Penny needs me."

On her way, Audra picks up *The Circus Elephant* book off the table and clutches it tightly.

"All I know how to do is be here for her. And if that's the wrong choice, hopefully we'll figure out the right choice."

Imaginary-Natalia wipes the imaginary tears from her eyes, "Lovely words!"

"Please," Penny begs, clutching onto Audra's wrist. "Let's get this over with."

"Sounds good to me," says Audra, trembling. "When you can, take in a deep breath and push."

Penny nods her head, takes a few breathes, grits her teeth, and obeys.

"If only I could tell you those things in real life," Audra thinks, so only her sisters can hear her.

"You should," says Imaginary-Kendra.

"Well, you should at least try," says Imaginary-Natalia. "We can't guarantee how we'll respond."

The two imaginaries giggle in harmony.

"Very good, Penny," Audra whispers. "Now push again.

Outside Audra's home on the beach, led by Norman, the Wise Woman and a few others run up Audra's ramp.

Norman reaches for the doorknob and then hesitates. "How do we know it's okay to go in?"

He turns to see the Wise Woman putting sterile white masks on the women's faces.

"Just be careful once we're in there, my little poppets," the Wise Woman tells them. "Be helpful. Be sanitary."

She puts on a mask of her own and opens the door.

They all rejoice to hear the cry of a brand new baby.

The ladies behind Norman ooh and ahh and skip through the door to see the baby.

Norman enters and watches the room with his back to the closed front door.

Blankets cover Penny as she rests on the bed.

Audra stands beside her, still as a statue, holding a beautiful baby boy in her arms.

Chapter 15: Hours of Silence

A still Audra stands in the middle of the busy room.

The other ladies whiz about, taking care of Penny, preparing the room for the baby, each of them peeking over Audra's shoulder as they pass by. Still, in the middle of that busy room, Audra remains in her motionless trance, as if the baby has cast a spell on her. She barely blinks. Her breathing is slow. Her smile seems permanently etched into her face. She stares into his dark eyes, massages his tiny hands, strokes his chubby cheeks, nuzzles his full head of hair, and rubs his floppy feet.

As she tickles his little lips, he gives her finger a little nibble.

For what seems the space of hours when it is really a matter of minutes, she lovingly holds the baby while the others race around her.

Eventually, the Old Wise Woman comes up beside Audra, places her arms around the baby, and lifts him away. With a gentle smile she says, "We need to take care of a few things, dear."

Keeping her eyes on the wee one, Audra's head swings swiftly round and slows down as if caught by gelatin. She follows him with poise and grace, appearing to move in slow motion.

While Audra circles them and the morning sun from the window warms them all, the old woman washes the baby's eyes, his face, and his little folds. Audra leans down and whispers into his perfectly formed ears, "I love you, little one."

"You can take him now," says the Old Wise Woman. Audra scoops him up like a handful of roses and whisks him over to his mother.

Penny, with joy in her cheeks and tears in her eyes, takes the baby and pulls him into her embrace. "I think he looks like an Adam," she says. Then she slips him, along with herself, under the covers to give him his first feeding.

Audra leaves them and saunters over to her bench by the window, where she continues her silent pondering. She watches the ocean's waves as the tide rolls in. She watches the undertow as it pulls the water out. Over and over, the waves crawl up the shore only for gravity to pull them back into the sea. Sometimes, they carry in bits of seaweed. Occasionally, they gift the sand with a seashell.

After the space of half an hour, Norman brings Audra the baby. She smiles at him briefly and turns back immediately to the island's newest circus cherub.

Baby Adam sleeps so peacefully as the next hour passes. For a brief moment, he opens his eyes. And when Audra peers into those deep, dark eyes, she silently gasps at all that she feels.

Poignant images from the best books she has ever read come flooding into the depths of her mind. She sees herself scaling the rocks of a castle tower to rescue baby Adam from the blazing flames, carrying him to the peak of an abundantly flowered mountain, uncovering gold and gems from the underground lakes of a cavern, leading the march of a noble army, nursing the poor beside Mother

Teresa, captaining a pirate ship through a turbulent storm, flying through the expanses of space, discovering new planets with life just like earth's, followed by new galaxies, each more impressive and colorful than the last.

And as her fanciful flight circles back to earth, to the middle of the ocean, in the thickest patch of greenery, on a small tropical island, she sees a familiar village of hidden circus people. And on the outskirts of that island, in the corner of a house on stilts, she sees a room with only four people inside, a wiry man standing beside a circular bed, an exhausted young woman resting there, and an older woman sitting by the window, trapped in a spell of stillness by a beautiful baby boy.

Everything she desires to be, every adventure she has wished to have, every feeling she has longed to feel, is there inborn in his untainted eyes.

"You remind me of someone," Penny says, drowsily looking up at Norman. "I'm not sure who..."

"Hopefully someone good?" Norman responds with his eyes on Audra.

"Are you in love with Audra? Is that why you followed her to this island?"

"Well, it might be dangerous to say ... If I say I love her, she might love me back, and who would I turn to then? We all need someone to care for, don't we? Maybe I'll stay here on this island and make sure you and this baby have a good life. That would be noble, wouldn't it? A man needs to feel noble at some time in life."

"William," Penny says, closing her eyes. "You remind me of my long-lost husband, William. But just on the outside. Just something about your jawline and your nose. Your eyes are different."

Norman looks down at Penny, who is now resting again. He walks over to Audra and puts his hand on her shoulder.

Audra eases out of her trance and smiles up at Norman. "I've never felt so much peace," she says.

She looks out the window to see the fishermen ships sailing off into the distance. A bit of anger toward them tries to wiggle its way into her heart, but she lets go of those harsh feelings. The current peace is too valuable to rehash something she can't control.

Norman lets out a long sigh.

"Oh, hi Norman. What is it?" Audra asks. "Oh yes, the Ringmaster."

Norman nods.

She bids goodbye to the baby then sprints most gracefully out her door.

Norman follows.

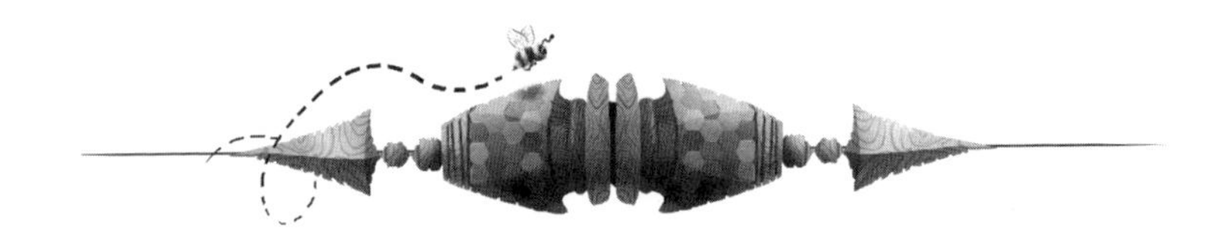

A dingy cloud of dust hovers in the Ringmaster's hot, muggy room. Audra opens the door slightly and peeks in. The Ringmaster lies bandaged in his bed. The Old Wise Woman and a couple of other people stand beside him. Andrew, the young man in a tiger-inspired costume, sits on the bedside.

"Stop saying that," Andrew cries. "You aren't dying."

"Maybe not, son, but I'll need you to carry on my legacy someday," The Ringmaster coughs, followed by a groan as he clutches his bandaged chest. "Care for this people, nurture them, do everything you can to keep them safe."

His eye catches a glimpse of Audra's peeking eye and he beckons for her to enter.

"Come in, Audra, I have a last request for you as well. You can have your machine back with no strings attached. I trust you will do the right thing. At least I hope you will."

Norman hops over and grabs the communication device from beside the bed.

Audra leaves immediately and paces about the porch.

Norman glances awkwardly at the people in the room.

"Just a moment," he says as he scrambles to go out after her. "What was that? You're not running away."

"Of course not," Audra says, pacing. She stops and faces the door. "Just gathering my thoughts." She takes a deep breath and marches in through the door.

"I'm taking you back to civilization," she

announces. The faces in the room turn to her in surprise. "Oh, and I'm taking Penny too. She can study engineering, I can help raise the baby, and you can get the best medical care I can find. "

The Ringmaster starts to laugh which soon becomes a painful groan. "Not happening."

"Nonsense!" Audra waves the other people in the room to action. "Get a stretcher ready to carry him to the beach. I'll have a helicopter here within the day."

"No, no, no..." The Ringmaster waves them to stop. "I'm not going."

"You must!"

"I never let anyone tell me what to do, and I'm not going to start on my deathbed."

"So just like that, you're just going to give up and die?"

"Look," says the Ringmaster, "I brought my people here. And here I'll stay with them. That's the decision I made when we first crashed on this island, and I won't change my mind."

Audra opens her mouth to speak, but the Ringmaster interrupts. "No discussion!"

Audra shouts, "Will you stop being dramatic so I can do something dramatic?"

"What?" the Ringmaster coughs.

Norman smiles.

"I'm taking you all back to civilization. I'll pay every expense. With your reef destroyed and your people dying for an audience, that is exactly what you all need. So I'm taking you back, and that's final!"

The Ringmaster lets out a pained chuckle as he

strains to sit up. "Really? "You'd do that for us? And what about those who refuse to leave?"

"Whether they stay or go, I will do my best to help. Though I hope at least you and Penny will come with me," Audra says, determined.

"It seems I misjudged you, Miss Audra. "The Ringmaster collapses back to his bed, breathing gently.

"As I have misjudged you," Audra smiles. "We should take a trip and start over."

The Ringmaster remains silent for a moment. The other members of the room look at him with concern until a smile appears, spreading his full beard outward. "Fine, fine," he says, still smiling. "I'll never hear the end of it until I say yes."

"Great!" Audra walks out with a giddy spring in her step. Norman gives an awkward nod to everyone in the room, then follows her out.

"Well done," Norman says as he catches up to Audra.

Audra nods and takes a deep breath. "Now! I need alone time and tea."

Chapter 16: Civility to Civilization

A helicopter descends toward the big white box, generating a whirlwind of sand and shells.

Audra, Norman, Penny, and the baby all shuffle down the ramp from the beach home. A group of circus performers passes them. All carry luggage on their shoulders.

"See you soon, apple dumplings," the Old Wise Woman shouts with a wave.

Audra waves back, "Yes, we shall." While they arrive at the helicopter and Audra waits for her turn to board, she looks down the beach toward a nice, large boat, where the Wise Woman boards and a few other circus members carry the Ringmaster over on a stretcher. Several other circus members wave at Audra from atop the boat. She waves back and climbs the ladder to board the helicopter.

The helicopter engine starts. It lifts, followed by the big white box, and the island shrinks away as they increase in altitude. As the individual trees blend into one great green mass, Audra watches from the window, hoping to spot the circus village from above. Most of the village remains hidden from view, but a few colorful dwellings pop out of the greenery.

Penny pats Audra on the hand, and they both look at each other and grin, looking forward to the new adventure ahead.

The rest of the trip, though it lasts more than a day, blurs into only a few minutes of memory: The musty ocean-liner where they fill up on gas, their arrival on a chilly-yet sunny morning, Norman opening their limo doors, A shower at the first five star hotel they can find, Penny's awe at the tall city buildings, a shopping trip for Penny's new clothes, and finally a university faculty portfolio review that ends in an accepting handshake.

When the limo finally arrives at Audra's home

in the middle of the city, Audra looks at her old house. "It's so much smaller than I remember," she whispers to Penny.

The real Natalia and Kendra, who've been waiting on the garden bench, stand and approach the limo together. Norman walks around and opens Audra's door. He reaches his hand down, and she quickly takes it and holds it for a long pause. She waits for him to return her gaze and when he does, she smiles warmly.

Norman starts sweating and appears to be suppressing an enormous grin. "Audra?"

Audra, suppressing an enormous grin of her own, can't think of anything to say, so she pats his hand and emerges. She continues holding his hand as she greets her sisters with a smile and a proper nod.

Natalia's jaw drops first, then Kendra's. Audra is obviously not the same woman they last saw: her clothes are the same but her skin is bronze, her smile is radiant, her hair is down, playfully waving about her shoulders, and most surprisingly, in her other arm she is holding brand new baby Adam.

Audra grins deviously, basking in the moment. These are precisely the reactions she had imagined. But the experience is much more gratifying in person.

Penny steps out and stands beside her, dressed in new clothes with peacock feathers still woven in her hair. The sisters look from Audra to Penny to Audra, apparently confused.

Norman snorts in amusement.

After Audra lets go of his hand, he holds it himself as if it were a precious treasure.

"Penny, these are my sisters. Kendra and Natalia," says Audra, breaking the silence. The four ladies exchange nods. "I've invited you all here for a tea party, and I expect you to all behave civilly. No arguments, only kind words."

Audra hands the baby to Penny and confidently walks toward her front door.

The others follow obediently behind her.

"Oh, and Kendra," Audra continues. "I will meet you at your gym on Saturday morning. Natalia and

I can visit the beauty parlor in the evening. And on Monday, I get some designated alone time." As she unlocks the door, she smiles back at them. "Sound good?"

"What has happened to you?" Kendra finally blurts out, still shocked in her observation of Audra.

"Yeah!" Natalia adds.

Audra smiles, keeping her response to herself until she's good and ready to share it.

"Oh," she says, "and I'm getting some new neighbors, you'll have to meet them." Audra leads them through her front door. "Better than the party animals who used to live there," she jokes.

Kendra and Natalia stop, look at each other, then walk a few paces backward. Just as they look at the house next door, a huge moving van pulls up. The back door flies up and several colorful circus people pop out, making delightful exclamations at sight of their new home.

Both sisters look at each other again and hurry in through the front door. Audra greets them and gestures for them to continue into the kitchen.

Audra emerges again from the front door, where

Norman waits eagerly "Would you please join us?" she asks him, reaching out her hand.

"Always," he says quickly, taking her hand and giving it a kiss.

"Thank you," she smiles, blushing slightly.

Norman nods at least five times as he passes her and heads into the kitchen.

"You're too kind to me, Audra!" comes the Ringmasters voice behind her. She turns around to see him in a wheeled bed complete with an IV and a friendly nurse to push him. He continues, "I thought you'd stick me in a hospital, not pay for special care in a brand new house."

"I keep my enemies close," Audra responds with a devious smile and a giggle under her breath.

The Ringmaster laughs nervously.

And at that, Audra returns to her home and shuts the door. She takes a deep breath and turns around, smiling at the empty room. She saunters into her kitchen, which overlooks the garden patio.

Kendra and Natalia sit around the table out there, chatting with Penny, cooing over the baby. Norman sits on the opposite side of the table and quietly observes.

As Audra silently watches the patio from her kitchen, she builds a cheese-and-cracker tray and boils a pot of water for their peppermint tea. While Kendra holds the baby, Penny skips into the kitchen and picks up the tray from Audra.

"Your sisters are lovely," Penny says as she leaves the kitchen.

Audra holds back a laugh and replies, "I hope so."

Penny peeks back in. "Thank you, again. For school, for the help, for everything!"

Audra nods and Penny smiles then rejoins the others.

Audra's face glows with joy as she watches her new family's interactions. She holds her heart, which pounds so joyfully that it seems about to leap from her chest. After finishing the tea, she remains there watching for several minutes, breathing in the silent beauty.

"Audra," Natalia calls out. "How's that tea coming?"

"Fine," Audra calls back, wiping a tear from her eye. She whispers to herself, "life is going to be just fine."

She takes the tray out to the table and sits beside Norman.

They laugh and talk together for hours.

And on the kitchen counter, printed on the last page of an open book, is the final illustration of Elphie, smiling in the warm embrace of her many monkey friends.

The End

A word from the Author/Illustrator:

Thank you for supporting and reading this book. When we Kickstarter-funded and self-published Vanishing Ink in 2014, I had no idea I would soon be animating at a studio where they asked for feature film pitches. I had hoped I would get to pitch it someday and was surprised to see the opportunity open up so quickly. It was a joy to be able to hand the studio heads an illustrated copy of the book, and I was even more thrilled that they considered the project for a time. Though they didn't buy my film pitch in the end, their creative V.P. offered her services as an agent for future developments.

I then moved to another animation studio where I pitched it again. Another studio invited me to pitch with them, and I've had several opportunities to pitch since.

Still, the biggest reward from Vanishing Ink has

been to hear how that book touched readers, and I hope this book does the same.

I started Cirque De Solitude before ever finishing Vanishing Ink because when I told people about the former book, they showed a bit of interest, but when I mentioned my circus story, they laughed with delight. Developing this book along with my animated short film, Layers, I learned and grew so much as a storyteller. It has undergone many revisions and improved drastically thanks to the excellent feedback from its first readers, especially Isaac Stewart, Travis Howe, and Rebecca Wiser. If we ever have the opportunity to make this into an animated film, it will undoubtedly undergo a further transformation to become the best film it can be.

Similarly, the illustrations, characters designs, and other embellishments serve as the visual development and inspiration for the even better images we will dream up for the big screen. I plan to continue developing books like this until we receive the funding for a full feature film. And whether that happens, I'll still enjoy making these books and short animations.

So thank you again for making this book a reality and supporting my projects. You are helping my dreams come true, and I get to entertain you in the process.

Thanks!

Scott Wiser

Important!

Don't miss out on my future books and animations!

Go to
scottwiser.com/follow

Or scan this with your camera app!

Thanks!

SILVER SUPPORTERS

Carl Sager

Quinn D. Woody

Here is special "thank you" to Emily Woody, who offered to do some last-minute proofreading.

Also, here's a shoutout to Christian Howard, one of the Kickstarter backers who purchased a cameo as the helicopter pilot in Cirque De Solitude. I did a sketch of him because: who would not want to sketch that beard?

GOLD SUPPORTERS

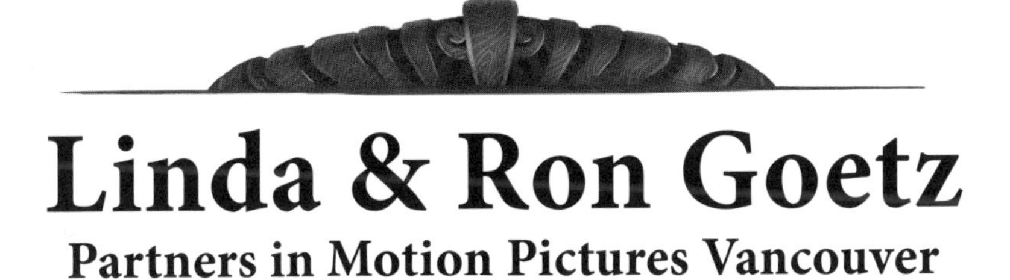

Linda & Ron Goetz

Partners in Motion Pictures Vancouver

GOLD SUPPORTERS

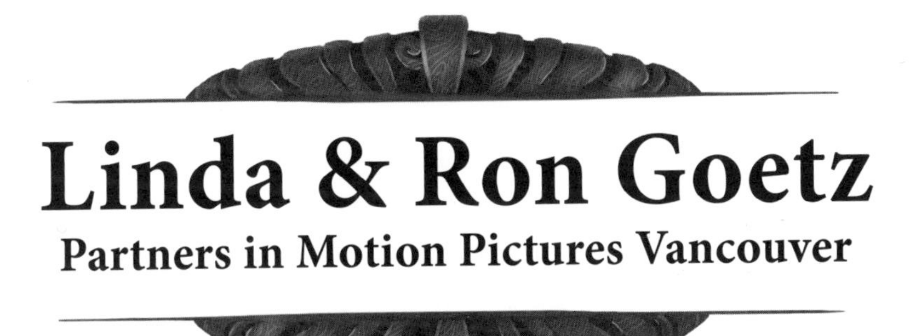